ROTATION
PLAN
EAST SU___ COUNCIL
WIT____WN
___AUG 2024

Night of the Gunslinger

With the town marshal laid up with a broken leg, Deputy Rick Cody must stand alone to protect New Town during a night of mayhem. At sunup Edison Dent will stand trial for Ogden Reed's murder and although Rick suspects that Edison is innocent, he also reckons his own sister knows more than she's prepared to reveal.

With Rick having only one night to uncover the truth, his task is made harder when the outlaw Hedley Beecher plots to free the prisoner while Ogden's brother Logan vows to kill Edison and anyone who stands in his way. Within an hour of sundown four men are dead. And so begins the longest and bloodiest night of Rick's life. . . .

Night of the Gunslinger

I.J. Parnham

A Black Horse Western

ROBERT HALE · LONDON

© I.J. Parnham 2013
First published in Great Britain 2013

ISBN 978-0-7198-0545-5

Robert Hale Limited
Clerkenwell House
Clerkenwell Green
London EC1R 0HT

www.halebooks.com

Typeset by
Derek Doyle & Associates, Shaw Heath
Printed and bound in Great Britain by
CPI Antony Rowe, Chippenham and Eastbourne

CHAPTER 1

Kirby Jarrett had disappeared.

For the last thirty minutes Deputy Rick Cody had followed him down New Town's main drag. He'd kept him in sight while never getting too close.

Kirby had wandered into saloons giving the impression he was looking for someone until he had appeared to accept he couldn't find his quarry and he'd headed to the station. But when Rick had looked around the corner of the station house, nobody was on the platform.

With his Peacemaker held low, Rick walked beside the station house wall. The door was open for a few inches, so he stopped and waited. When he heard nothing he pushed the door fully open.

The room had only one grimy window and, as it was sundown on this dull winter day, the interior was shadow-shrouded. He counted to five and then went in low.

The retaliation he'd feared didn't come. When he

pressed his back to the wall beside the door he saw only a table in the centre of the room, and several chairs. He still checked behind the door and beneath the table, but Kirby wasn't here.

So, while considering where his quarry had gone to ground, he headed out onto the platform, but then Kirby barged into him, knocking him into the wall before he dropped to his knees.

He just had enough time to register what had happened. Then he pushed off from the platform.

He had yet to gain his feet when Kirby kicked his chin and sent him sprawling onto his back. With his vision whirling, Rick raised his gunhand, but the hand moved up unusually quickly.

Only then did his befuddled senses tell him that when he'd fallen over he'd dropped his gun.

'You weren't sneaky enough,' Kirby said with confidence. 'I knew you were following me.'

Rick shook his head and blinked several times until he could focus on Kirby's form standing over him.

'No matter,' Rick said. 'You shouldn't have returned to New Town.'

Kirby shrugged. Then he drew his six-shooter and aimed down at Rick's chest.

His eyes narrowed with a look that said he was about to fire; so, in desperation, Rick rolled to the side while scrabbling around for his dropped gun.

He had yet to locate it when two rapid explosions of gunfire sounded. Rick looked up, surprised and relieved that Kirby hadn't shot him, but it was to see Kirby stumbling to the side.

Then Kirby walked into the wall, where he grabbed hold of a notice board. The board failed to support his weight and it peeled away from the wall, making him drop to the platform and onto his back.

Beyond his form stood a man, his hat pulled down low, his long coat, which brushed the platform, spread open to reveal his drawn gun. A tendril of smoke rose up as he moved forward to stand over Kirby.

He stared at Kirby's pained face, which protruded out from under the notice board. Then he hammered lead repeatedly into his body.

'You were right,' the man said as the last gunshot echo faded away. 'He shouldn't have returned to New Town.'

'Who are you?' Rick murmured, lost for anything else to say.

'My friends call me Logan,' the man said. Then, with a last glance at Kirby's body, he turned on his heel and walked away.

Norton Wells never turned away a customer, but this afternoon he was minded to make an exception.

The newcomer had a patch over one eye, and ridged scars had ruined half of his face. He stood in the mercantile doorway looking outside as if he expected he'd been followed.

Then he sidled up to the counter with his gaze set

firmly on Norton while his right hand was buried deep beneath his coat in a way that suggested he was clutching a weapon.

'What do you want?' Norton asked. He leaned on the counter with one hand lowered so that he could quickly reach the hidden rifle he kept close to hand.

'Put both hands where I can see them,' the man said. His one eye flitted its gaze down to look at the counter, accurately picking out where the rifle was lying.

'Who are you?'

The man glanced around the mercantile before he leaned forward in a conspiratorial manner with his head cocked to one side. Accordingly, Norton too leaned over the counter, but then he wished he'd been cautious when the man whipped his hand from his coat and metal gleamed.

A knife appeared and the man thrust it up until the point jabbed into the skin beneath Norton's chin.

'I'm George Fremont.' His one eye narrowed when Norton shrugged in a bemused manner. 'I work for Hedley Beecher.'

Norton raised his chin from the knife, but when he didn't reply, George raised the knife to again jab it into Norton's chin. This time Norton couldn't crane his neck any higher to avoid the point.

'Everyone's heard of him,' Norton murmured.

The newcomer grinned, revealing an arc of yellowed teeth.

8

'They have, but only you know what he wants.' George waited, but Norton didn't volunteer an answer. So he inched the knife higher, forcing Norton up onto tiptoes. 'We figured out you have the map. Hand it over or I'll cut you the biggest smile you've ever made.'

Norton gulped, the motion making the knife pierce the skin. Damp warmth slithered down his neck and to his vest.

'You've made your point.' He offered a smile that made George sneer, and then gestured to the back store.

George kept the knife held firmly for several seconds, then he lowered it encouragingly downwards.

'No tricks,' he whispered. 'You have one minute.'

Norton gave the biggest nod he could manage. Then, when George rolled over the counter to stand at his shoulder, he led him into the back store.

Norton stopped a few paces beyond the doorway and looked around. No good ideas came for a way out of his predicament, so he settled for the only option he could think of. He headed to a huge corn sack that he had dumped on a high shelf.

Norton reckoned he wouldn't be able to move it without making the shelf collapse, but it had been lying there for a month, so it might provide a convincing subterfuge.

'I put the map in here,' he said, patting the bulky object.

'Bring it down,' George said, eyeing the large sack dubiously.

For his ruse to work Norton reckoned he had to act confidently. So, eager to please, he clambered onto a lower shelf, grabbed the sack, and tugged. The contents had settled and the sack didn't move.

After apparently struggling for several seconds, he drew himself up onto the shelf beneath the top one. He tugged again and grunted loudly, seemingly straining every sinew, while only pulling lightly.

'I can't move it,' he said between gasps.

'Step aside,' George muttered, becoming exasperated with his failure. He moved in and raised the knife to a gap in the shelving.

He had pressed the blade to the bottom of the sack when Norton gave up his pretence. He drew the sack up, then tipped it over.

At the last moment George saw what he was doing, but he was too late to stop the sack slapping him in the face and knocking him over onto his back.

The shelf creaked ominously and then rocked forward, but when Norton jumped down it righted itself with a clatter. Then Norton was on George, pinning him down to the floor beneath the sack.

A well-placed knee on George's wrist kept the knife from inflicting damage. Then he bore down on the sack with his chest, this time not holding back.

George struggled and shouted, his voice muffled beneath the bulky sack, but quickly his efforts became weak. Norton didn't move, sure that relenting for even a moment would give his opponent a chance to turn the tables on him.

Five minutes passed before he pulled off the sack to reveal the scar-faced man, his patch lying askew to reveal the full horror of his burnt face.

Norton stepped back, planning to leave the body so that he could explain the situation to Deputy Cody. Then he noticed the bulge beneath George's coat. He opened the coat and jerked backwards in surprise.

The lining had ribbing that secured wads of bills. He estimated that George had $500 secreted about his person.

Norton hurried to the door and peered up and down New Town's main drag. Few people were about and none of them was paying any attention to his mercantile. George hadn't even left a horse outside.

He put that surprise from his mind and, when he returned to his storeroom, he was clutching an empty saddle-bag.

CHAPTER 2

'You did well,' Marshal Hannibal said when Rick Cody had told him who was lying beneath the blanket, although he cocked an eyebrow when he removed the blanket from Kirby Jarrett's form.

'That wasn't my doing,' Rick said.

While Hannibal hobbled back across the law office to his desk, Rick detailed events after he'd recognized Kirby's face from one of the wanted posters devoted to Hedley Beecher's outlaw gang.

'And you've never seen the man who saved your life before?' Hannibal asked, his voice gruff.

'No.' Rick replaced the blanket over Kirby's body. 'So if you've got no more questions, I'll go find him.'

Hannibal leaned on his desk as he caught his breath after his exertions, although he took longer than Rick thought necessary to reply.

'I don't want you to talk to him tonight.'

Hannibal didn't meet Rick's eye. Instead he

glanced at the door and then manoeuvred himself into his chair. Then he raised his splinted leg onto a second chair and fussed over the broken limb until he was comfortable.

Last month Hannibal had broken his leg. At the time Rick had been a barman in his brother-in-law Jasper Snyder's saloon, the Lonesome Trail. Jasper's old friend Edison Dent had returned and, as he always did on his frequent visits, he'd regaled everyone with tales of the town's history.

Tunnelling had made the original mining camp at Old Town dangerous, so when the mine had been worked out, the people who had remained had built New Town a mile away. With the benefit of the railroad, the town had flourished and Edison had prospered too.

After one too many whiskeys Edison had claimed he'd ridden with Hedley Beecher, the leader of an outlaw band that last year had raided $10,000 in silver from the train on its way through New Town.

When Marshal Hannibal heard about the boast Edison had retracted his story. Afterwards, in the Lonesome Trail's private gaming room, Edison had played poker with Jasper, the marshal and two other old friends from Old Town, Norton Wells and Carl Schmidt.

They had enjoyed a jovial night until Jasper had accused Edison of cheating. Edison had protested his innocence, but even though the pot had been only ten dollars, Jasper had told Ogden Reed, the man who kept the peace in his saloon, to throw him out.

Later that night Ogden had been found shot up, lying over the poker table. Despite the lack of witnesses, Hannibal reckoned Edison had killed him. While he pursued his own leads, he had deputized Rick to lead a posse.

The posse had scouted around fruitlessly and, when they returned to town, Edison was behind bars and Hannibal had a broken leg, courtesy of a fall in Hollow Cavern while apprehending Edison.

With Hannibal incapacitated, Rick had stayed on as his deputy and for the last month the marshal had slept in the law office. The strain had soured his mood, so Rick wasn't perturbed when the marshal scowled at him.

'You mean,' Rick said, 'you want me to stay here until tomorrow's trial?'

'No!' Hannibal snapped. He sighed and took a deep breath. 'I deputized you to help me deal with Edison, but you knew I'd have to decide if I could justify employing you permanently.'

'I know,' Rick said. Hannibal's low tone suggested that he wouldn't like his decision, but he pressed on anyhow. 'But your break's a bad one. You won't be able to sit a horse for another month. You still need a deputy.'

'I do.' Hannibal coughed. 'But that man isn't you.'

Rick couldn't think of a suitable reply and so a minute passed until the uncomfortable silence was broken by the door opening. Todd Snyder, Rick's young nephew, wandered in and, adopting his usual manner, he leaned against the wall with his hands in his pockets. His arrival made Hannibal smile.

'Him?' Rick said, unable to hold his silence or keep the surprise from his tone.

Hannibal nodded. 'I intend to appoint Todd as my new deputy. I'd be obliged if you'd spend time with him tonight and show—'

'You can go to hell,' Rick muttered.

'I know you're angry,' Hannibal said, 'but you still have your duties to perform and they won't end until the circuit judge arrives tomorrow.'

When Rick didn't reply immediately, Todd spoke up.

'Can you two work this out?' he whined while staring in horror at Kirby's shrouded form lying beside the door. 'It's dinner time and I'm hungry.'

Rick gave Hannibal an exasperated look and, now that his anger had worn off, he accepted that Hannibal wouldn't have employed Todd on his own volition. This was his sister's doing.

'One man's been killed already today. As Kirby was connected to Hedley Beecher, I don't reckon he'll be the last. You need a competent deputy.' Rick waved a dismissive hand at Todd, struggling to find the right words to describe him. 'You don't need a kid who's more interested in his next meal.'

As he'd said everything he wanted to he turned to the door before Hannibal could reply.

He planned to walk away, tell his sister what he

thought of her meddling, and never return to the law office, but before he reached the door pattering footfalls sounded outside. A breathless man hurried in while pointing back over his shoulder.

'Come quickly,' he shouted. 'I've found a body in Norton Wells's mercantile.'

'You're doomed,' the drunk man shouted. 'We're doomed. The whole town's doomed!'

Logan leaned over his whiskey and tried, as the other drinkers in the Lonesome Trail were doing, to ignore the distraction. But the newcomer jostled his elbow, spilling his drink across the counter; when Logan turned to him the man was waving his arms, oblivious to the mess he'd made.

Logan waited until an arm swung towards him. Then he grabbed the wrist, yanked down hard, and turned the raving man so that he bellied up to the bar.

Several customers murmured their support of Logan's action, letting him learn that his captive was Carl Schmidt, a babbling fool who owned the Lucky Star saloon. With his free hand, he pushed Carl's face down so that his nose dipped into the pool of whiskey.

'The whole town's not doomed,' he muttered in his ear, 'but you sure will be if you don't apologize real nicely.'

Carl squirmed frantically, his nostrils blowing bubbles in the whiskey, but Logan held his arm firmly, so that he slumped against the bar.

'Get off me,' Carl whined, his voice strained because of his contorted position. 'I've come to warn you. I've seen them. They're coming for you. They're coming for us. They're—'

'Annoy someone else,' Logan snapped, but he couldn't stop Carl babbling and, with a desire to get this pointless confrontation over with, Logan dragged him away from the bar and then pushed.

'It's them,' Carl shouted, stomping to a halt. He raised a finger and pointed across the saloon room, his manic eyes rolling. 'They're here!'

With an exasperated sigh Logan refilled his whiskey glass, but a gunshot roared, making him swing round. Carl was cringing, while in the doorway a man stood with a raised smoking gun in hand.

Carl met Logan's gaze, calmness replacing his pre-vious wild behaviour. He offered a wan smile that said he had tried to warn him. Then he dropped to the floor and knelt, with his hands over his head and his body hunched over so that his forehead touched the floor.

Logan turned to the guntoter, who had already lowered his six-shooter to pick him out. As the rest of the customers peeled away to leave clear space between them, Logan settled his stance. He held his glass casually against his chest so he could reach for his gun if he got the chance.

'What do you want?' Logan asked, keeping his tone light.

'Kirby Jarrett was shot up at the station. He was looking for me.'

'Then I'm sorry you missed your appointment.' Logan waited until his disarming comment made the man narrow his eyes. Then he raised his glass in a salute. 'I'll finish my drink now.'

He turned and leaned on the bar, putting his weight on his left elbow. He figured that with so many witnesses, the man wouldn't shoot him in the back, so he looked forward, hoping to catch sight of him in the mirror behind the bar.

'Don't turn your back on me,' the guntoter snapped. Although Logan couldn't see his reflection, his voice came from a few paces in from the doorway.

Logan made an obvious gesture of moving his glass to his lips and then down. This time he heard a footfall as the man came closer and, through the mass of people, he saw the man's reflection edging forward.

He turned to the nearest customer and hunched his shoulders, the action masking his placing the glass on the bar. When the weight left his hand, he slipped his hand down. Then he jerked around sharply while crouching, his gun coming to hand.

He'd picked his moment well, as the man was glancing at Carl who was gesturing towards the stairs. The distraction meant his gun was no longer aimed at Logan.

Logan made him pay for his mistake and an explosion of gunfire tore out. Hot lead slammed into his opponent's chest.

The man squeezed out an involuntary shot that cannoned over Logan's shoulder and into the wall, but by then Logan was firing again. With time to aim accurately, he delivered a shot to the man's forehead that cracked his head back. The man swayed and then keeled over.

Logan dismissed him from his thoughts and hurried over to Carl.

'Obliged,' he said, kneeling at his side.

'You're still doomed,' Carl said. Fright widened his eyes. 'We are. Everyone is.'

Carl beckoned with a finger for Logan to come closer. When Logan leaned over him the finger straightened, then jerked to the side.

The gesture was the same one as he'd made earlier, so Logan turned quickly. Carl had picked out a man who was climbing the stairs to the saloon's upstairs rooms. He was walking stealthily while the customers looked at Logan and Carl.

The man registered with a flinch that he knew he'd been noticed. Then he threw his hand to his gun. He'd managed only to draw when Logan's deadly shot slammed high into his chest, making him fold over. Then he stumbled and, head over heels, he tumbled down to the bottom of the stairs, where he lay still.

'Any others?' Logan asked.

Carl sighed and then relaxed. Logan took that to mean he'd dealt with the danger, so he moved back to the bar and let the customers deal with the after-math.

While four men took the two dead men away, their matter-of-fact manner suggesting this wasn't an unusual occurrence in the Lonesome Trail, Logan sipped his whiskey.

He poured his new friend a drink, but when he didn't join him, he glanced over his shoulder and saw Carl beating a hasty retreat to the door. A moment later the hubbub in the saloon room silenced and someone stepped up to the bar beside him.

Logan flicked his gaze to one side. He blinked hard in surprise before he smiled.

A woman had come to see him and her piercing blue eyes, pleasing smile, and tightly drawn-in skirt told him that she was Virginia Snyder, joint owner with her husband of the Lonesome Trail.

'Two dead men in here,' she said, her lilting tone seemingly amused, 'another one at the station, and Carl Schmidt venturing in here for the first time in a month. You've been in town for only an hour. I wonder what could happen in the next hour?'

'That depends,' Logan said, smiling, 'on whether I'm in your company or not.'

She giggled. Then she leaned closer, drawing his eyes down to her low-cut bodice.

'Finish your drink and then join me,' she whispered in his ear before flicking her gaze to the stairs. 'Don't keep me waiting. I get bored quickly.'

Then she turned away and, with a slow sashaying walk that drew the gaze of every man in the saloon, she headed to the stairs.

CHAPTER 3

Norton Wells took a deep breath, slicked down a wayward lock of hair, and then raised a tentative hand to rap on the door.

To his surprise, a moment later the door was thrown open and Virginia Snyder appeared. She considered him with a sneer before raising herself to look over his shoulder and down the corridor.

'Oh it's you, Norton,' she said with a distracted sigh. 'Go away. I'm expecting an important visitor.'

She moved to close the door, but Norton jumped forward and wedged himself into the gap.

'Would that visitor have anything to do with all the shooting in town?' he asked. 'I hear that—'

'Nobody cares about anything you hear, least of all me.'

She considered the door and his form placed squarely in its path. With a bored sigh, as if the matter was no longer worth worrying about, she raised her hands and walked over to a dresser. She sat and applied a layer of rouge, although to Norton's eyes her cheeks were already adequately coloured.

Norton reckoned this was the nearest he'd get to an invitation to enter her room, so he shuffled in and closed the door behind him.

For a while he enjoyed watching her performing a task. Then the thought came that this was the first time he'd ever been alone with her.

An involuntary cough rose from deep in his chest. He fought it down, but that increased the pressure in his chest until with an explosion of noise a racking, wet cough tore out followed by several more as he fought to clear his throat.

When he'd stopped coughing and he'd wiped the spittle from his chin, she was staring at him with her lip curled in horror. Then she shook her head sadly and picked up a pitcher of water and a mug.

She filled the mug and then backed away quickly, as if she expected him to start coughing again, but the water eased his throat and, in an odd way, despite the embarrassment, Norton felt more relaxed.

'Thank you,' he said, handing back the mug. 'That was very kind.'

She glanced at the door, suggesting that she'd now dismiss him, but instead she sat down and leaned back with her legs crossed. She arranged her bell-shaped skirt to display her petticoats.

'Why are you here?' she asked as a trim calf emerged through a previously unnoticed split in the material.

She waited for an answer, but the sight of her knee and the knowledge that he'd already spent more time in her company than he'd expected meant Norton couldn't remember the speech he'd rehearsed back in his mercantile.

'I wanted to see you,' he said lamely.

'You can see me every night in the saloon room.'

'But your husband barred me from the Lonesome Trail last month. He said he didn't want me annoying you no more.'

'I know, but that's not stopped you looking through the window, has it?' She folded her arms, the motion hitching her skirt and revealing more of her leg above the knee. 'Which raises the question of how you sneaked in here tonight.'

'Nobody stopped me.' Norton gestured at the door as he struggled to make this meeting play out in the way he'd hoped it would. 'Are you waiting for one of your many admirers?'

She giggled and fluffed her hair. 'I am, and he's sure to be more entertaining than you're being.'

She cocked her head to one side clearly expecting a retort, but when Norton didn't reply immediately, she stifled a yawn behind a lace kerchief.

'I admire you,' Norton said, at last remembering one of the things he'd wanted to say. With his confidence growing, he became aware of the comforting weight in his jacket pocket.

She must have noticed his change of attitude as she sat up straight and then uncrossed her legs before standing. She paced across the room to stand before him.

'I know about your feelings for me,' she whispered. 'I've known since the day Jasper brought me to New Town and you and all your other little friends couldn't believe that a man like him could bag a woman like me. But there's a small problem: I have no interest in you.'

She planted a finger on his chest and pushed, her gentle motion making Norton stumble backwards.

'But you should.' Norton took a deep breath. He knew he shouldn't reveal everything, but he had to dangle an intriguing hint. 'I have secrets.'

That comment proved to be too oblique for the fickle Virginia and her gaze again drifted to the door.

'We all have secrets, and I'm sure yours are of no interest to me.'

She was wrong, but he smiled. 'And I have money, lots of money. I can help you.'

She snorted with disdain. 'What you call a lot of money is not what I'd call—'

She broke off to utter an excited squeal when Norton withdrew a handful of bills from his pocket.

'You were about to say?' Norton said, his heart pounding.

She bounced on the spot, backed away, swirled around twice, then came forward with a huge smile on her red lips.

She raised her arms to rest the wrists on his shoulders. Then she ran the back of a hand across

Norton's cheek, her touch the softest he'd ever known.

'I was about to say,' she purred, 'that a man like you could interest me, after all.'

'You don't like me, do you?' Todd said when he and Rick were approaching Norton's mercantile.

'I don't,' Rick snapped. 'You've taken my job, not because you'll do it well, but because of your parents.'

'You'd be nowhere without my mother helping you out.'

Rick had expected this reply, but it still irritated him.

'I tended bar for her for five years,' he said. 'If that's somewhere, I'd prefer to be nowhere.'

Todd didn't reply and the two men moved on down the boardwalk. When they headed into the store, they found the body lying on its back behind the counter.

The face was contorted and the clothing was askew. Two furrows cut through a layer of corn husks on the floor and led into the back store, where Rick found a discarded sack. He considered it while Todd loitered in the doorway staring at his boots with his upper lip curled in disgust.

Then Todd shuffled on to join Rick. He looked around the room with the casual air of a potential customer.

'How long do we have to stay here?' he grumbled

while rubbing his stomach.

When Rick ignored the question Todd finished considering the room and, presumably because he hadn't noticed anything he wanted to eat, he headed to the door. He glanced at the body, shivered, then sat on the counter.

Rick went back into the main room. While fingering the sack, he considered the body's suffused features, which were made even uglier by the ridges of scar tissue on one cheek and the black hole of the empty eye-socket.

'My sister may have talked Marshal Hannibal into employing you,' he said with a softer tone than before, 'but you have no interest in this work, so why did you accept?'

Todd winced. 'Because the alternative was worse.'

Todd slapped his legs and then, without offering an explanation, he jumped down and stood at Rick's shoulder, although he still looked everywhere other than at the body.

Rick pressed the sack into his hands. 'Keep hold of this. You'll need it later.'

'Why?'

'Because if you want to avoid that alternative, you'll have to write a report on this incident and you'll need to describe the murder weapon.'

Todd flinched, then held the sack at arm's length; this revelation piqued his interest for the first time.

'You're good at this,' he said, smiling. 'I'd thought you were only good at keeping secrets.'

Rick had been nodding, thinking he had impressed the importance of the work on Todd, but the last comment made the anger that had been gnawing at his guts since Hannibal had sacked him bubble over.

'Where did you hear that?' he demanded, clutching Todd's jacket and pushing him back against the counter.

'What you annoyed about?' Todd murmured, cringing. 'I just meant my mother trusts you.'

Rick held on to him for a moment longer, unwilling to concede that he'd overreacted. Then he shoved him away and pointed at the body.

'This dead man,' he said, his voice gruff, 'is depending on you to find out who smothered him. You reckon you can do that?'

To Rick's surprise, Todd stood tall.

'I might. For a start, I know who he is.' Todd smirked when Rick raised an eyebrow. 'He's George Fremont, a member of Hedley Beecher's outlaw gang. I saw his wanted poster in the law office.'

Rick appraised the body. George's poster wasn't as prominent as Kirby's was, so he hadn't made the connection. He considered Todd without disdain for the first time.

'He's the second man connected to Hedley to die tonight,' Rick mused before he cast a grim smile towards Todd. 'And you might make a lawman, after all.'

*

'My wife's busy,' the voice said through the open doorway. 'But you can talk with me.'

Logan had heard about what had happened to Virginia's husband, so he was already looking down when he went into his room. Last year Jasper had fallen in Hollow Cavern, crippling himself for life.

Now he was sitting at a writing desk in a chair that had two large wheels on either side. With impressive dexterity, he wheeled himself backwards and then turned to face Logan.

'I've gathered from your barman,' Logan said, 'that she wants to hire me to keep trouble away from your saloon, and that the previous man she hired was killed last month.'

'The dangers of the job shouldn't worry a man who's killed three times already today.'

Logan shrugged. 'I'm not worried, but that's only because I keep myself alive, not others.'

'My wife can be persuasive.'

Jasper waited until Logan frowned. Then he beckoned him to follow and, turning the wheels slowly to avoid making a noise, he wheeled himself across the room to a panel that was set into the wall at his head height. He gestured and, getting his meaning, Logan slid the panel aside to reveal two round holes.

When Jasper backed away, Logan lowered his head to the holes. A moment before his gaze focused on the scene in the adjoining room he heard enough to know what he'd see, but by then it was too late to stop himself looking.

He flinched away to meet Jasper's amused smile. Quickly he put the panel back in place.

'You don't mind?' Logan asked.

Jasper patted the chair and then his legs, which were as stiff as the wooden chair-frame.

'Since my accident, I'm only half a man. If you'd finished your drink ten minutes earlier, you'd have been in there.' Jasper winked when Logan balked in horror. He wheeled his chair back across the room. 'Later tonight, it could still be you. My wife gets bored quickly, but she never gets tired.'

'I won't get caught up in your twisted lives. I have other matters to deal with.'

Logan turned to the door, but Jasper coughed, making him stop.

'Even if you don't want to sample what my wife will offer you freely, tonight has proved that Edison's trial will be a dangerous time. She'll still pay generously for protection.' Jasper chuckled. 'And whatever she offers you to carry out her wishes, I'll double it to do mine instead.'

'Nobody plays games with me,' Logan muttered, rounding on Jasper.

'Then you've come to the wrong place,' Jasper said, unconcerned by his anger. 'When you've thwarted whatever dangers come our way, she'll make you an offer to kill me.'

'And you want me to kill her instead?'

'No. I want you to ignore her.' Jasper considered Logan's incredulous expression and spread his hands. 'Since my accident, the only pleasure left to me is foiling my wife's every move.'

'In that case,' Logan said in a resigned tone, 'I'll accept your offer, and hers.'

'Obliged.' Jasper held out a hand, but Logan didn't take it.

'But I don't want your money,' he said.

Jasper nodded without a flicker of concern. He wheeled his chair back and forth until he'd aligned himself with Logan.

'What are your terms?'

'Only one.' Logan waited, but when Jasper considered him placidly, he accepted that, despite appearing to know plenty, Jasper didn't know who he was. 'Ask me for my full name.'

Jasper narrowed his eyes. 'What's your name, Logan?'

Logan met Jasper's gaze, searching his eyes for his reaction.

'I'm Logan Reed, Ogden's brother.'

CHAPTER 4

'I'm pleased you came back,' Marshal Hannibal said.

Rick made his feelings clear by walking slowly past what had once been his desk to the stove.

'Unlike your new deputy,' he said, 'I have a sense of duty and pride. I'll stay on until the judge arrives tomorrow. Then I'll kick your good leg from under you and walk out of here, never to return.'

Hannibal uttered a supportive laugh, but Rick only scowled at him, unwilling to lighten his aggrieved mood.

'And where is my new deputy?'

'Martha's Eatery. Apparently the strain of pretending to be attentive for fifteen minutes exhausted him.'

'Todd's not as stupid as you make out. He might overhear something useful.' Hannibal considered Rick's dubious expression and then continued: 'While you were gone, the gunslinger Logan shot up two more men in the Lonesome Trail. They also worked for Hedley Beecher.'

'That means my sister will need me, so I'll see out my last hours in the Lonesome Trail.'

'She won't need you. She's hired Logan for protection.' Hannibal licked his lips. 'With a gun like that behind her, she'll be squealing with delight all night.'

Rick pointed at him. 'My sister annoys me, but that doesn't mean you can insult her. I was joking about kicking your good leg away, but make one more comment like that and I'll do it.'

Hannibal lowered his gaze and Rick poured himself a coffee, now feeling unwilling to go to the saloon.

'Then try this: I need you,' Hannibal said, his voice low. He glanced at the grille in the corner of the office, then pointed at a plate of hard bread and even harder cheese. 'Edison's due his meal and my leg's hurting real bad. I don't reckon I can get down there.'

Rick put his mug back on the stove and treated Hannibal to a sarcastic grunt of thanks for admitting he needed him. Then he collected the plate and took it to the grille.

He had visited the jailhouse only once before and that was shortly after Hannibal had locked up Edison. Since then, Hannibal had dealt with him, his twice-daily ritual of overcoming the slippery steps being one he entrusted to nobody else.

The law office had been built over a cavern of the

kind that had first attracted miners to Old Town. The only entrance was a chimney over which the grille had been set. To date, no prisoner had ever escaped.

Once he'd raised the grille, Rick paced down the circular steps that had been carved into the rock and then onto the wooden steps that took him down to the base.

The cavern was forty feet across, although only the central section was high enough for a man to stand comfortably. Four cells had been placed under the lower section, adding to any prisoner's discomfort.

Accordingly, Edison was lying on his cot staring up at the oppressive ceiling of rock a few feet above his head. He moved his head to consider Rick and a small smile appeared, as if he'd expected him to come. Then he returned to looking upwards.

'Your meal,' Rick said, sliding it under the bottom bar.

'Obliged,' Edison said. 'Are you enjoying a pleasant last night?'

Rick smiled. 'Hedley's plans have been thwarted. Four bodies are lying out there.'

'Four, eh?' Edison shrugged, then shuffled off his cot. With his head down, he moved over to the plate and looked up at the grille. 'But I was talking about you no longer being a deputy.'

'How do you know that?'

'If I'm quiet and the people up there are angry, I hear everything.'

Rick shrugged. 'It was only ever a temporary

appointment.'

Edison picked up the plate. This time, as he moved back to his cot, he stood straighter than before, so that his head was a finger's width from the ceiling, showing how the time he'd spent down here had let him judge the cavern height perfectly.

'Good,' he said when he'd sat down. He poked at his bread and gnawed off a mouthful, his expression intense. 'Because I have plans for you.'

Rick folded his arms. 'You're a prisoner with no contact with the outside world other than Hannibal and me. You don't have plans. Other men who work for Hedley had plans, but they got nowhere, not with my sister's new hired gunslinger looking after the Lonesome Trail.'

'I wonder how she'll pay for his services?'

Edison tore off a mouthful of bread with his teeth. His quick motion suggested that the news had annoyed him and that he wasn't as confident as he wanted to appear.

'That's none of your concern. You should think only of your trial tomorrow.'

Edison chuckled and looked up, his eyes eager.

'I won't stand trial.'

'Hedley won't break you out.'

'He won't need to.' Edison shuffled up to a sitting position on his cot and gestured at Rick with the last piece of bread. 'Later tonight, you'll return and free me.'

Rick was familiar with Edison's flights of fancy, but

he couldn't hide his surprise at this claim.

'Why would I do that?'

'Guilt.' Edison placed the bread on his plate, then threw the plate to the floor, where it rolled along, spilling the last pieces of bread and cheese onto the floor. 'Before sunup, you'll face four trials: of air, fire, water and finally earth. Each trial will be tougher to survive than the last one and so, to avoid the final trial, you'll free me.'

'Have you lost your mind?' Rick spluttered, watching the plate roll to a halt in front of the bars. 'You're not behind what's happened today, never mind anything so bizarre.'

'Except your trials have already begun. As you survived the first, you know I'm serious.' Edison smiled when Rick shook his head. 'Haven't you noticed how oddly people are looking at you?'

Rick collected the plate and turned away, but he'd reached the steps when he recalled that Todd had avoided looking at him. He was a strange young man, but Hannibal had also found it hard to look him in the eye and he never shied away from confrontation.

'They have,' he said, rounding on him. 'So stop talking in riddles.'

While grinning, Edison mimed removing a hat from his head and considering it. When he didn't explain, Rick slipped his own hat off and then winced.

The crown sported a hole, the edges dark and fraying. When he thought back, he recalled hearing

two gunshots when Logan had shot Kirby Jarrett.
Clearly Kirby had fired at him, but he hadn't aimed
so accurately.

He stuck a finger through the hole and judged
that if the bullet had been an inch lower, it would
have parted his hair. Another inch lower and it would
have ended his life.

'That was your trial by air,' Edison said. 'Your next
trial by fire won't be so easy to survive. So, will you
release me now to avoid it?'

Rick opened his mouth to pour scorn on Edison's
opportunistic use of his lucky escape, but then he
thought better of it. He put his hat back on.

'Have a pleasant last night,' he said. 'I won't return
to free you. The next time you see me, I'll be giving
evidence.'

Rick turned away smartly, hoping to avoid further
taunts, but Edison leapt from his cot and slammed
into the bars, making them rattle.

'You won't,' he shouted. 'You'll free me because
you have a conscience. You know I didn't kill
Ogden.'

'Goodbye, Edison,' Rick said.

He set off up the steps, clattering his feet on the
wood to make it hard for Edison to shout taunts at
him, but he had to pause when he moved off the
wood onto the slippery rocks.

'Worse,' Edison said, his voice low but loud
enough to carry, 'you know who really killed him and
if I stand trial nobody can stop me speaking the

truth. I'll destroy your sister. You and your family won't be able to stay in town after I reveal what she's done and what she wanted me and then Ogden to do.'

Rick hurried up the steps. When he'd clambered up into the law office, he kicked the grille back in place.

'He had plenty to say,' Hannibal said in a bored manner that suggested he had heard them talking although he hadn't heard the specifics.

'He always has,' Rick said between gasps, his heart still pounding and not just from his quick climb up the stairs. 'But then again, down there that's all he can do.'

'So you knew my brother, Ogden Reed?'

Rick flinched and then looked up to find that the gunslinger Logan had joined him in Martha's Eatery.

For the last ten minutes he had worried his pork around the plate while dwelling on his conversation with Edison. So, welcoming the distraction, he gestured to the chair opposite him.

'I did,' he said. 'After Jasper's accident he worked in the Lonesome Trail.'

'Until Edison shot him up.'

Rick frowned and, when he couldn't think of a suitable reply, Logan used his silence to order a plate of salted pork, beans and rice.

Back in the jailhouse, Edison had been right. Rick knew that Ogden had given his sister more than just protection and he'd heard them arguing on the night of his death, so he suspected she knew more than she was prepared to admit.

Long before Ogden had arrived in town, Edison had been close to his sister too and Rick had heard the rumour that she'd wanted him to kill her husband. Despite this, he still hoped that Edison had killed Ogden because of the events at the poker table and that his sister hadn't been involved.

Either way, Edison's defence was sure to have a devastating effect.

'Edison will be tried in the morning,' Rick said when the meal arrived. 'I assume that's why you're here.'

'Sure.' Logan forked up some beans and gave a sly smile. 'And you should be thankful that I am.'

'I've got mixed feelings. More people have died in New Town since sundown than in the last year.'

Logan shrugged. 'Kirby was about to kill you and the other two came looking for me.'

'And the man in Norton Wells's mercantile?'

'I've not been to a mercantile.' Logan aimed the fork at him with a warning gesture. 'Don't pin the blame on me for everything that happens here.'

'I won't, but that's the trouble with vendettas; eventually you cross the line.'

Logan chewed his beans thoughtfully, then carved a thick slice of pork.

'Should I take that as a warning?'

'You should, but after tonight I won't be a deputy.

The marshal has a new man.' Rick waited until Logan raised an eyebrow in surprise, then pointed to the corner of the room. 'See that man?'

'You mean the snoring kid with his feet on the table and his hat about to fall off his head?' Logan smiled when Rick nodded. 'If he'd been the deputy following Kirby, I wouldn't have bothered saving him.'

Rick snorted an appreciative laugh. 'If he'd been the deputy, Kirby would have been following *him*.'

Logan laughed. Then the two men ate in companionable silence. Rick finished his meal first.

'Nobody saw your brother being killed, but Ogden threw Edison out of the saloon earlier that night. It's likely he'll be found guilty and I'd guess he'll get a life term.'

'He won't serve it.' Logan leaned back to glance at his gun. 'I have a more appropriate justice in mind.'

'As I'll be a lawman until sunup, I should warn you not to carry out the cold-blooded murder of a man in custody.' Rick sighed. 'So I'd be obliged if you'd tell me your intentions.'

'My intentions are to finish my meal.' Logan forked another mouthful and then chewed quietly. 'Then I'll head back to the Lonesome Trail where I'll protect Jasper Snyder while fighting off the amorous intentions of his insistent wife.'

'I wish you luck. It won't be an easy job, both halves.'

Logan smiled. 'Ogden succeeded with the first

half, but I wonder how long he resisted the second half?'

Rick leaned back in his chair and tipped back his hat.

'I could tell you, but ask Virginia.' He waited until Logan frowned. Then he lowered his voice. 'She's my sister.'

Logan winced, for the first time losing his confident demeanour.

'I hadn't made the connection,' he murmured.

Rick shrugged. 'You're not the only one who hasn't made enough connections yet. I reckon there's more going on here than just a simple matter of Edison Dent killing your brother after he'd been involved in an argument over a poker game.'

Logan snarled and gripped his fork tightly, showing that he wanted the situation to be a simple one that he could resolve by killing Edison.

His anger made Rick wonder if he should mention his theory about his sister's involvement, but before he could decide, Norton Wells rushed into the eatery and hollered for everyone's attention.

'Fire!' he shouted. 'There's a fire in the Lucky Star saloon.'

The remainder of Norton's explanation was drowned out by the clattering of plates as the diners abandoned their meals and bustled to the door.

The only customer to loiter was Todd, who stretched and yawned after his sleep. He avoided catching Rick's eye as he cleared half-emptied plates onto his own before he shuffled back behind his table and began eating.

Rick considered him with disdain as he mingled in with the crush of people who were pushing their way outside. As he approached the door, the smell of burning came to him.

'So Edison was right,' Rick murmured to himself. 'It's time for my trial by fire.'

CHAPTER 5

People were milling about on the road when Rick and Logan reached the edge of town.

The Lucky Star saloon was the oldest building in town. It had once stood some distance from the Old Town mining camp and, when the settlement had moved, it had continued to serve customers. But since Carl Schmidt had started raving it had fallen into disrepair and it was now a ramshackle building that had looked ready to collapse.

Rick judged that the fire would consume the whole building but, as the Lucky Star lay on the edge of town, he reckoned the fire wouldn't spread.

Flames were flickering through broken panes in one of the two downstairs windows, but the door was free of flame and several people had edged forward to peer through it. Then they waved at the crowd with calming downward gestures, conveying that everyone had got out.

'If nobody's in there,' Norton shouted, pushing

people aside to get closer to the saloon, 'stay back and let the fire run its course.'

The people ahead of him didn't argue and they moved back to a safe distance. With the situation appearing calm, Rick made his way through the throng to join Norton. Logan followed on.

'You the first to see the fire?' he asked.

'Yeah,' Norton said, his eyes wide with excitement as he waved his arms. 'I was drinking with Carl when the fire started in a back room. We threw water on the flames, but a whiskey barrel burst and the flames spread. Everyone ran.'

'After all the trouble here,' Logan said with a smile, 'you should have stayed in the Lonesome Trail.'

Norton gulped, but when he didn't reply, Rick shook his head.

'You shouldn't go in there, Norton,' he said. 'You were barred, which means that's the second time you've acted oddly today. Earlier, a body was found in your mercantile.'

Norton fidgeted nervously, then turned to watch the fire, his gaze wide-eyed as he made a clear effort to ignore the deputy. After waiting a few seconds for him to reply, Logan grabbed his shoulder and spun him round.

'Answer the deputy's question.'

'He's not a deputy no more,' Norton said with downcast eyes.

Rick batted Logan's hand away and slapped his

own hands down on Norton's shoulders.

'How do you know that?' He waited, but when Norton didn't react he shook him and drew him up close. 'Marshal Hannibal only told me two hours ago and he doesn't leave the law office.'

'The word's spreading,' Norton murmured. He glanced up, but he couldn't meet Rick's eye, so he looked past him. Then he brightened. 'But I'll answer the new deputy's questions.'

Rick looked over his shoulder to see Todd mooching towards them while watching the fire with the smiling wonderment of a child.

'I doubt he'll have any, ever.' Rick released Norton and beckoned Todd over. 'What's your advice, Deputy?'

When he arrived, Todd shrugged in his usual bored manner and then pointed at the saloon.

'I'm just wondering,' he said, 'what Carl Schmidt is doing up there.'

All three men swirled round. Todd had pointed to the upstairs window on the side of the building, but nobody was visible there and the watching townsfolk weren't paying that window any attention.

'Carl's not outside,' Norton murmured, peering at the crowd. Then, with tentative steps, he edged closer to the saloon.

While Logan asked nearby people if they'd seen the owner, Rick followed Norton.

'When did you last see him?' he asked.

'He was in the saloon room when the fire started,'

Norton said, staring up at the window with a horri-
fied expression. Then he shook off his surprise and
hurried on to the saloon.

Rick ran after him, but the flames were flicking
through the window and he had to take a detour to
reach the door. Norton showed no such caution and,
with an arm up to shield his face, he braved the
searing heat and reached the door within seconds.

Rick turned and caught Logan's and Todd's attention. In a moment Logan took off after him while
Todd decided this was a good moment to start ques-
tioning people.

At a run, Rick followed Norton inside, where he
had to cringe away from the heat on the bar side of
the saloon. Tables steeped in spilt liquor had caught
alight while the relatively open saloon area was free
of flames.

Despite that, thick smoke was building up below
the ceiling and the wind coming in through the
window and door was fanning the flames.

Within minutes the building would be an inferno
and yet, thirty feet ahead, Norton was skirting
around the bar on a foolhardy mission to reach the
stairs.

'He sure has got guts,' Logan said when he joined
Rick.

'I don't know where he found them,' Rick said. He
pointed out the route Norton had taken to reach the
stairs. 'He's always been a snivelling, money-grabbing
snake who's been as welcome in a saloon as this fire.'

46

'I wonder what gave him confidence.' Logan chuckled, as if he knew the answer, then set off along the route Rick had indicated.

At his heels, Rick reached the stairs without mishap, but one glance at the saloon room made him stop.

The fire was now creeping towards the doorway. Two men were trying to battle their way in, but then they thought better of making the attempt and they backed away.

With his misgivings making his stomach churn, Rick paced up the stairs. Within a few steps he moved into a patch of swirling smoke that cut visibility down to a few feet.

A worrying crash sounded near by, but his eyes were watering and he couldn't see what had made the sound. When he reached the top of the stairs, he would have turned back if Logan hadn't kept going.

After another few paces he emerged into clearer air and saw an open door ahead. He hurried on to the doorway, where he found Logan loitering. He soon saw the reason for his hesitation.

Baking heat blasted out from the bedroom, searing Rick's skin and making him feel that he'd be roasted if he moved even a few feet forward. Smoke was rising up through the floor and, halfway across the room, Norton was cringing back against the wall with his hands to his face. In front of him was a hole where the floor had fallen away.

Beyond the hole Carl lay in a hunched heap,

presumably having succumbed to the heat and smoke.

'Get back,' Rick shouted. He paused to cough. 'We'll never save him. If we don't go now, we'll never get out ourselves.'

He didn't add that their chances of escaping were already slight, but his desperation registered with Logan, who rocked forward and then back, clearly torn about trying to reach Norton.

For his part Norton registered that he'd been called only with a quick glance at them. Then, with a roar of defiance, he stepped backwards for a pace, then ran and leapt.

He made it over the hole. When he landed on the other side he went to his knees and tumbled into Carl, who didn't react to being hit. Then desperation fuelled Norton on as he leapt to his feet, grabbed a chair, and launched it at the window.

Glass was still falling away as he grabbed Carl and dragged him to the window. He struggled to get him there, so Logan and Rick edged forward; but with every pace that took them closer to the hole the heat intensified.

The flames below were now licking at the edges of the hole and Rick felt the heat rising up through his soles.

By the time Rick could see down into the saloon room, Norton had stood Carl up before the window where the cool air made him stir. With him starting to help Norton, Rick slapped Logan's shoulder and then hurried back to the door.

When he looked out of the room, a rolling mass of smoke was filling the top half of the corridor and flames were scooting along the old carpet that trailed down the centre of the floor. He backed away, coughing and spluttering, and his concerned expression told Logan everything he needed to know.

They turned back and watched Norton help Carl to roll over the sill and disappear from view. Then Norton glanced back at them before he followed him out.

Rick listened, but the flames were roaring below and he didn't hear either man land outside.

'On the count of three,' Logan said, the words coming between painful-sounding wheezes. 'Run, jump, and then keep going through the window.'

'Sure,' Rick said, although the word emerged as a croaking cough as the smoke clawed at his throat.

Logan eyed the hole, from which the far edge peeled away exposing yet more of the flame-filled lower room.

'Three,' Logan said. Then he set off. He took four long paces and then leapt.

Rick thought he'd struggle to leap over the expanded hole, but he covered the gap easily and landed only a pace away from the window. His momentum nearly tumbled him outside, but he didn't follow his own advice. He stopped and held out a hand.

Heartened, Rick ran for the hole. With every pace

the heat intensified and unbidden a pained screech tore from his lips, but he reached the hole and leapt towards the window.

The floor collapsed beneath his feet, spilling him forward.

He suffered a terrifying vision of the flames below beckoning him on to an agonizing death. Then he slammed down on his side on the hot floor.

He slid along, the wood creaking and bowing away beneath him as it threatened to collapse. Then a hand slapped around his wrist.

Gratefully he locked hands with Logan and let him draw him to his feet. Here, the air from outside was sweeter and cooler than anything he'd ever breathed in before.

It also fanned the fire inside.

When he looked back, flames were licking at a chair beside the door. Then a smouldering blanket burst into flame.

'Time to go,' Rick said and slapped Logan's arm.

Logan wasted no time in sitting on the sill: he glanced down and then dropped. Rick followed, pausing for just a moment to let Logan get out of the way.

He dropped, seeing nothing through his watery-eyed vision other than the after-images of the burning room. A moment later he slammed down into the soft earth. He tumbled onto his chest, feeling jarred but otherwise intact.

Then, while blinking rapidly, he looked around

for Logan, finding him sitting up and grinning mani-acally after surviving their brush with death.

A second surprise came when Todd arrived and held out a hand.

'Norton and Carl are safe and fine,' he said.

Rick couldn't bring himself to accept his help and he waved him on to Logan, who let him draw him to his feet.

Then the three men shuffled out of the alley and headed into the throng of watching people, the heat that seared their backs driving them on.

They kept going until they reached the middle of the road, where they slumped down to kneel on the ground and watch an inferno that was now raging out of control.

'Norton sure was brave,' Logan said as a wall gave way and crashed to the ground, sending up a shower of sparks that was brighter than the starry night.

'He was,' Rick said. He looked around for him. Carl was sitting up and Todd was explaining what had happened, but Norton wasn't to be seen. 'Which is very odd indeed.'

CHAPTER 6

Only when Norton Wells reached his mercantile did he stop to catch his breath. He leaned back against the wall outside and dragged in deep gulps of air as he tried to remove the taste of smoke from his mouth.

It took him five minutes before he could breathe normally, but his heart didn't stop thudding loudly. He was just too elated.

Tonight's activities had been more exhilarating than even his most lurid dreams. Before he'd been barred from the Lonesome Trail, exchanging a few words with Virginia had kept him happy for days. Afterwards, just the sight of her outside had kept him content.

But tonight he'd spent an hour in her room and he'd become her trusted confidant. Even better, she hadn't wanted to know about the secrets he'd guarded for the last month, only about him.

The only sour note had come when he'd headed

to the Lucky Star to boast to Carl about his exploits. Carl had been even less lucid than usual; then the fire had broken out.

Emboldened by the night's activities, he'd rescued Carl and now he felt he could achieve anything. A new life beckoned, filled with private meetings with Virginia, becoming her business partner, them starting a new life together. . . .

While whistling a merry tune and with the flickering flames on the outskirts of town lighting his way, he went inside, but the moment he lit a lamp that tune died out. Someone had been here while he'd been away.

George's body had been discovered, but that hadn't alarmed the deputy and he hadn't blamed him. But the scene inside didn't reflect that calmness.

Sacks had been strewn around, crates had been opened, and shelves had been toppled.

'Who did this?' Norton murmured to himself.

He didn't expect an answer, but when he slipped into his back store to survey the chaos, an arm slapped around his chest from behind and drew him backwards into the shadows.

'We did,' a voice muttered in his ear.

Norton struggled until a hard object, presumably a gun, jabbed into the middle of his back.

'What do you want?' he asked.

'The same thing George Fremont wanted, except we've heard he's dead.'

'I don't know what you . . .' Norton trailed off as

men moved in the shadows.

They closed in. Despite the gun at his back Norton reacted decisively, as he had done earlier.

He jerked forward, taking his captor by surprise, and tore himself free of his clutches. Then he doubled back and ran through the door to the counter, which he leapt onto and then over.

He landed on the other side bent forward and used his momentum to propel him across the mercantile. With his arms wheeling he leapt over fallen items until he reached the door. His head was still thrust down, so he only saw someone step into his path a moment before the man grabbed his shoulder and stayed his progress.

Then his assailant swirled him round. Five men were coming through the door to his back store, their actions slow and confident.

Norton squirmed, but this time his assailant had gathered a firm grip and even though Norton dug in his heels, he was walking across the room with ease. Then a second man joined the first and grabbed his legs.

They deposited him on the counter and pushed him down onto his back. One man held his shoulders down while another held his legs.

'Did you enjoy watching the fire?' a man said from the darkness. 'If you did, we can torch your mercantile too.'

'Please, no,' Norton murmured.

'Then I'll ask you again: where is it?'

'I told you,' Norton whined. 'I don't know what you want.'

Metal flashed in the low light and a knife was placed above his head. Then it was moved lower.

Cloth ripped as his vest front was torn open. Then the flat of the blade was placed against his chest. The coldness made him squirm and a third man moved out of the shadows to hold him steady.

Norton gulped when he saw that this man was Hedley Beecher.

'Then I have bad news,' Hedley said with a grin. 'This is going to be a very long night for you.'

'Don't worry,' Logan said, taking Virginia's arm to stop her carrying on down the road to the Lucky Star. 'The fire's being left to burn itself out.'

'Where's my son?' she asked. She struggled to free herself as she peered past Logan at the flames that still lit up the edge of town.

'He's a deputy lawman now. He can't have his mother running around after him.' Logan smiled, but she didn't return it so he lowered his tone to a serious one. 'Todd has a fine knack of avoiding trouble. He's gone to the law office and he's not even slightly singed.'

Virginia shot him a grateful look and stopped trying to wrest herself free.

'And Rick?'

'He's keeping everyone away from the flames. He's fine too.'

She nodded, then turned to go back to the Lonesome Trail.

Logan joined her and they walked in silence. By the time they entered the saloon, she'd regained her composure. With an ingratiating smile and a raised eyebrow, she invited him to join her at the bar, but Logan made for the stairs.

'We've not had our private chat,' she called after him. 'It's not too late yet.'

'Your charm won't work on me,' Logan snapped with more vehemence than he'd intended. Embarrassed at his outburst, he stopped at the foot of the stairs while she moved over to the window.

'How have I offended you?' she asked. 'Has my brother told you tales about me?'

'We were too busy dealing with the fire to talk.'

'And you'll probably remain busy until the trial ends. All I ask is that you spend time with me.'

'Edison Dent is standing trial tomorrow for killing the last man who spent time with you.'

She shrugged. 'Ogden was special to me, but he certainly wasn't the last.'

Logan sneered. 'Your husband deserves better.'

His insult only made her turn and smile. She ran a finger down the window and then considered the dust she'd removed before wiping her dirty finger on her palm.

'He knew what I was before he brought me to New Town and, before last year, he enjoyed the benefits. I still like to think that despite his accident I can please him.'

She lowered her head and squinted, confirming she knew about the holes in the wall.

Logan had anticipated the tactics she'd use to win him over, but honesty hadn't been one of them. He joined her at the window where they both watched the fire.

'I hate people who hide their true intent,' he said after a while, 'so I won't lie to you. I'm not interested in your welfare, or your husband's. I'm Logan Reed. Ogden was my brother.'

Her sharp intake of breath didn't sound feigned. While she was still off guard he grabbed her shoulders and swung her round to face him.

'And you've come here,' she breathed while suppressing a sob, 'to find out the full truth about his death?'

'Sure. Your husband promised to help me unearth any facts that the trial misses. Can you better that?'

She licked her lips, seemingly regaining her confidence and, with a growing smile, she raised her arms to sweep his hands aside. Then she rested both wrists on his shoulders.

'I was the last person to see Ogden alive, apart from his killer, of course.' She brushed his cheek with the back of her hand and lowered her tone to a husky whisper. 'So shall I tell you what we were doing during our last hours together?'

'Do you know how the fire started?' Marshal

Hannibal asked when Rick returned to the law office.

'Nobody saw anyone acting suspiciously,' Rick said, 'so it was probably an accident.'

Rick didn't look at the grille in the corner as he forced himself not to dwell on Edison's prediction that he'd face a trial by fire.

Hannibal nodded. 'The fire probably saved Carl's saloon from falling down.'

'I agree,' Rick said, as another worrying thought hit him.

Today Jasper's saloon, Carl's saloon and Norton's mercantile had suffered trouble. Last month, these men and the marshal had taken part in the ill-fated poker game with Edison.

'Todd told me what he did.' Hannibal's neutral tone suggested he hadn't made the connection. 'You must be proud of him.'

'I'm more impressed than when you appointed him, which isn't hard.' Rick glanced around the deserted office. 'Where is the fearless deputy now?'

Hannibal frowned. 'His mother took him home. He's getting some well-deserved rest.'

Rick snorted a laugh. 'That was always likely to happen.'

'After he saved your life and all those other people, you shouldn't be sarcastic.'

'During the fire he avoided being useless, for once, but me and Logan took all the risks.'

Hannibal shrugged. 'I wouldn't have expected that attitude from you. Perhaps it proves I was right to put my trust in Todd.'

Rick stared at Hannibal, amazed that he'd take this view. Although he'd decided he'd keep his dignity by seeing out his term of duty, he had to clench his hands into fists to stop himself tearing off his star and throwing it at the marshal.

'I wish you luck,' he said through gritted teeth, 'with a kid whose only talent is to be elsewhere when he's needed.'

'Except Todd's more observant than you. He noticed that none of the dead men had horses and the train passed through three days ago.'

As his hands were aching, Rick set them on his hips.

'That means they were in hiding, possibly like Edison out at the old mine workings. Nobody would ever find them in the miles of tunnels under Old Town.'

That suggestion made Hannibal glance away. As he said nothing more Rick headed to the door. Outside on the boardwalk a steady drizzle was starting up, promising that the recent heavy rains might return again tonight.

'Two trials passed,' he said to himself, holding out a hand to cup the water. 'Water to defeat next.'

He took deep breaths and, when that brought the whiff of burning to his nostrils, he slapped a fist against his thigh, deciding that he'd no longer accept other people controlling his life.

If he was to prove one way or the other whether his

sister had been involved in Ogden's death, he could-
n't wait until Edison did his worst at the trial. He had
to uncover the truth himself beforehand, even if he
had only one night in which to do it.

As he reckoned that everything that had happened tonight was connected to Ogden's death in a
way he couldn't see yet, he turned his mind to the
night's other mystery: who had killed George
Fremont?

As Norton Wells had been involved in both inci-
dents, he headed for his mercantile.

Norton was always open for business, but the
building appeared deserted. Rick slowed and made
his way cautiously to the only window.

He peered through. Inside a shielded light
burned. It'd been set on the floor and five men were
sitting around it.

The men were companionably passing around a
liquor bottle while playing a game of chance that
involved a variation on the three-card trick with three
mugs and a coin.

They appeared to be in good spirits, but the room
had been ransacked, crates and sacks having been
thrown around. Rick's gaze fell on the counter where
Norton lay. He wasn't moving and an arm covered
his face.

Rick turned from the window, meaning to burst in
through the door and surprise them, but a man had
edged into the doorway. He had already drawn and
now aimed a gun at him.

'What are you doing here, Hedley Beecher?' Rick asked, recognizing him from the likeness on the law office's most prominent wanted poster.

'You don't ask the questions,' Hedley said. He gestured with his gun, directing Rick to head inside.

As the gun was aimed away from him Rick used the moment of distraction to leap away from the building. He hit the boardwalk on his side, then rolled under the hitching rail and onto the hardpan.

Hedley blasted a shot at his tumbling form that kicked splinters from the corner post. Rick took refuge behind the limited cover of the post. Then, firing blind, he loosed off a quick volley of shots.

His gunfire was ill-directed and it peppered through the window. A moment later sounds of consternation erupted inside, followed by rapid footfalls as Hedley backed away seeking his own cover.

As the rest of the men joined Hedley, Rick ran with his head down. Hedley's men hurried him on his way with a rapid burst of gunshots that tore into the boardwalk and the wall, but before they could get him in their sights he gained the corner of the building.

While punching in bullets, he ran down the dark alley beside the building to reach the next corner where for several seconds he listened. Men shouted and bustled, but the sounds came from the front of the building and nobody appeared.

Rick reckoned that despite the darkness reducing the advantage of his superior numbers, Hedley wouldn't stay back for long. He had only moments to rescue Norton.

He hurried to the back door. He'd been in the storeroom earlier, so despite the low light level he picked a route across the storeroom easily and reached the internal door.

The solitary light illuminated the main store area, so he risked slipping inside. During his quick perusal, he didn't see anyone other than Norton.

When he moved closer to the counter he confirmed that Norton was still breathing, but his bared chest glistened and he was groaning, seemingly oblivious to Rick's rescue attempt. He shook Norton's shoulder, making Norton try to push him away weakly.

'It's me, Rick,' he whispered.

While Norton grunted in reply, Rick heard Hedley deliver an urgent order from somewhere nearby.

Norton must have heard him too as he stopped fighting him off. So Rick took his arm and guided him to jump down from the counter. Then he turned him to the back store.

Norton could barely stand, so Rick wrapped an arm around his shoulder. Then, with a slow, stumbling gait they headed to the door.

Outside, the drizzle had become more insistent. Rick kept going, unmindful of his direction other than to ensure that they moved away quickly. Only when his arm started aching from supporting Norton's weight did he let up.

He let Norton slide to the damp ground. Then he knelt beside him and listened, but he could no longer hear Hedley and the other men.

'Obliged,' Norton murmured. He tried to raise himself, but then he thought better of making the attempt and lay down on his back.

Despite the poor light, the movement let Rick see the full extent of his injuries. His chest was a patchwork of cuts and his wild eyes showed the panic he'd suffered during his torture.

'Tell me what Hedley wanted,' Rick said, offering him an encouraging smile, 'or the next time he comes for you I'll leave you to enjoy his tender care.'

'The map,' Norton gasped.

His voice was weak, so, figuring he'd pass out soon, Rick spoke quickly.

'Did he get it?'

Norton's eyes closed. Rick slapped his cheek in irritation and then repeated the question. Norton's eyelids fluttered before he considered him.

'He reckons he's the only one who knows the way now. But I fooled him. I made a copy. And it's safe now.' His voice was faltering as if he were speaking in a dream. Then his eyes closed, this time with heavy finality. 'Nobody will ever find it.'

'Where is it?' Rick demanded. When he didn't get an answer other than a prolonged groan of pain, he persisted with the other important and unanswered question. 'What does the map show?'

'Secrets,' Norton murmured. Then he moaned,

the sound a low keening whine of a wounded animal that became fainter until his head flopped to the side.

CHAPTER 7

'Are you all right?' Virginia said, concern watering her eyes as she emerged from her room.

Rick had wanted to reach Todd's room without meeting her. So he moved on, forcing her to hurry from her door to block his path.

'It's been a busy night,' Rick said. He looked past her down the corridor to Todd's room. 'I need to speak to your son.'

'After braving the fire, he's retired for the night. Don't disturb him.' She considered his stern expression. 'I know you're angry with me, but you can come back to the Lonesome Trail and tend bar.'

'I'd sooner starve.'

'Except you won't. You're a resourceful man, but being Hannibal's deputy is perhaps the only hope Todd has.'

Rick couldn't disagree with her last comment. After rocking back and forth on his heels several times he relented and joined her in her room.

'I'm surprised you found work for him,' he said, 'that'll put him in danger frequently.'

She shrugged. 'He isn't interested in the saloon, and he has to do something.'

Rick forced himself to smile. 'You're hoping he'll hate working for Hannibal so much he'll show an interest in the Lonesome Trail.'

She winked and leaned towards him. 'For that, or for anything else. I won't have him wasting away his life.'

'And as a result, you cut me out of your life.'

'I didn't know Hannibal only wanted one deputy. I thought he'd keep you on and you could teach Todd how to survive.' She gripped his arm briefly and lowered her voice to an honest-sounding tone. 'Please believe me.'

Rick frowned. 'Then I will, but it doesn't make the result of your interfering any easier to bear.'

With that problem discussed, she sat at her dresser and considered herself in the mirror.

'What will you say at Edison's trial?' she asked, raising her chin to stretch her neck.

'The truth. And you?'

'The same, although I don't know much.'

'Nobody would expect you to.' Rick smiled thinly. 'After all, you didn't kill Ogden Reed.'

'I didn't.' She returned his smile. 'But sometimes you look at me as if I did.'

Rick sighed, her response giving him a chance to ask the question that worried him the most.

'You argued with Ogden that night and I'd heard rumours about what you wanted him to do.' He took a deep breath. 'So I know you're hiding something and that's making my job harder when I have only one night to find out if there's another explanation.'

He searched her eyes, but the veiled accusation didn't appear to cause her any concern.

'We all have secrets.'

'I don't. I saw Ogden go up to your room. In the morning he was lying dead on the poker table, and men who go to your room at night don't usually leave.'

'They all do, eventually.' She gulped and hunched over. The shadows made her face look lined and sagging. 'Admitting that in court will be harder for me than admitting I spent most of the night with a man who wasn't my husband.'

Rick frowned. 'Edison will defend himself by attacking you. If our family is to have a future in New Town, your testimony will be vital. Make sure your version of events is a good one.'

Her eyes flickered, confirming that she hadn't told him everything. He turned to the door quickly. As he left he felt her gaze on him, but he didn't look back.

When he reached the end of the corridor he knocked on Todd's door. Todd didn't reply so Rick edged the door open. To his disgust, Todd was lying fully clothed on the bed, snoring.

Rick slipped into the room and stood over him, amazed at his nephew's behaviour even allowing for his low opinion of him. Then, with a snarl, he grabbed his legs and dragged him off the bed.

Todd landed on the floor with a thud and a groan. He waved his arms in irritation, as if he'd accidentally fallen out of bed, and tried to clamber back. Then he noticed Rick.

'What are you doing here?' he murmured around a yawn.

'I could ask you the same.'

'Marshal Hannibal told me to rest. Tomorrow will be busy.' Todd got to his feet and considered Rick, with his hands on his hips. 'And now that I think about it, what's that got to do with you? Hannibal's my boss, not you.'

'Hannibal's got a broken leg and he's not going nowhere, whereas I can teach you to stay alive. Thanks to your mother, I've got only one night, but I'll do my best.'

Todd gave him a sceptical look that said he doubted Rick could instil survival instincts in him even if he had a year.

'I guess that means you won't let me go back to sleep.'

'You guess right, and you can please me again by telling me what you did with the sack you took away from Norton's mercantile.'

'Logan Reed asked for it, so I gave it to him.'

Rick looked aloft, feeling both surprised and elated. Norton had said the map was now safe, and Rick had guessed he'd hidden the copy in the sack, but it sounded as if Logan had reached the same conclusion.

Todd was looking longingly at the bed, so Rick pointed at the door.

'Then we have work to do and it shouldn't present a challenge to the man who rescued all those people from the fire.'

As he shuffled out of the room, Todd had the grace to look ashamed.

First they went to the doctor's surgery. Norton Wells hadn't regained consciousness, but Doctor Grant reported that Logan had come to see him.

The only other patient was Carl Schmidt, who looked weary and battered after suffering from smoke inhalation and then being bundled out of an upstairs window, but that didn't stop him beckoning them over with an eager wave.

'I'm doomed,' Carl croaked when Rick approached his bed. His eyes rolled with manic glee. 'You're doomed. We're all doomed.'

'Did Logan Reed talk to you?' Rick asked.

Carl shuffled round to lie on his side. 'He's doomed too.'

Rick decided that was a confirmation. 'What did you talk about?'

'He can't save himself. You can't. I can't.' Carl pointed at Todd and winked. 'He'll be fine.'

Todd didn't react. He had already grown bored with the conversation and he was eyeing an unoccupied bed with interest.

'Where did Logan go?' Rick said.

'Away, and that means his fate is now sealed.' Carl waggled a finger. 'Tonight, he will face four trials.'

Rick flinched, having not expected that answer. He sat down on the nearest bed so that he didn't tower over Carl.

'Of air, fire, water and earth?'

Carl giggled. 'And one will kill him, as one will kill you, as one will kill them all, as one did kill the others.'

'Who was killed by a trial?'

'Last year a trial by air killed Jasper Snyder,' Carl said in a surprisingly calm tone. 'Last month a trial by water killed Marshal Hannibal. Tonight, a—'

'Both of those men are still alive,' Rick snapped, getting to his feet.

'So I predict that tonight,' Carl said, carrying on regardless, 'that a trial by fire will kill Logan and a trial by earth will kill you.'

Carl leered and pointed at him, eagerly awaiting a reply that Rick couldn't find. When he stayed silent, Carl dismissed him with a shrug and then looked at the ceiling.

'That man's a fool,' Todd said when Rick left the bed.

Rick smiled. 'It's frustrating when a fool's the only person who has information you need, isn't it?'

Todd opened his mouth to reply, but when the insult registered, he flinched.

'That's not fair.'

'It is. A man who was friendly with your mother was killed. At the trial tomorrow his killer will say things that'll make her life difficult. She's relying on you to make sure that doesn't happen.'

'My mother's friendly with lots of people,' Todd said in an unconcerned manner that showed he hadn't understood what Rick had meant. 'Nobody will think badly of her.'

Rick sighed. 'You're a lawman, Todd. Start acting like one.'

'I am. I've answered all your questions.'

'Except for the one I needed you to know of: where's Logan gone?'

'Then that's where you're wrong.' Todd raised his chin proudly. 'I saw what was drawn on the inside of that sack. I know what interested him.'

With a quick gesture Rick directed Todd to go outside. Then he closed his eyes and counted to five slowly before he followed on behind, muttering to himself.

Outside, the rain had become so heavy he could no longer see the buildings on the other side of the road. He found Todd kneeling on the edge of the boardwalk. He'd found a stick and was sketching on the hardpan between two puddles.

Rick sat beside Todd and watched him produce a series of small circles and a large uneven circle, all of which were connected by straight lines.

'Are you sure this is what you saw?' he asked when Todd straightened up.

71

'I've got a good memory,' Todd said proudly, 'and I can use it when people stop shouting at me.'

Todd leaned over the map and made marks beside several circles. These symbols soon filled with water: there were five crosses of differing sizes, but only one star and that was beside the topmost circle.

'The Lucky Star saloon?' Rick mused.

In a giddy moment that made his eyes become unfocused, he saw what the map showed.

The large, irregular circle was a representation of New Town. This meant that most of the smaller circles depicted the old mine workings in Old Town, along with Hollow Cavern. The thickest line was the underground river that emerged into Hollow Creek; that probably meant that the lines connecting the circles were tunnels. Several lines travelled from the mine to New Town.

Rick took the stick away from Todd and marked a large cross over the starred circle. Then he set off for the edge of town. This time he didn't care if Todd followed, but the young deputy pattered along docilely after him.

The insistent rain was now dampening the remnants of the fire, leaving just a few obstinate planks smouldering away. Only one corner of the structure was left standing.

Someone had already rooted around in the debris: Rick reckoned that man was Logan.

He stepped into the debris and, after confirming that it had cooled enough to walk through, he gingerly made his way around the burnt timbers by picking out the puddles of water.

He saw nothing that hinted at an entrance to a tunnel that nobody other than the original miners knew about, so he turned back, taking the most direct route to the road. This took him across an area of unburnt wood where rain had collected.

He moved on to this area slowly, but the wood still creaked ominously, making him stop. While he sought out a different path, the slick of water on the wood drained away.

The water disappeared faster than he'd have expected and he stared at the wood for several seconds until he saw why.

Set within the wood was a square area. When he stood over it he saw that it was a trapdoor. He used the standing corner of the building to orient himself and decided he was behind the saloon room.

He beckoned Todd, but his brief period of being useful appeared to have exhausted him. He was standing hunched in the rain with his hat drawn down low, staring down the road at the Lonesome Trail.

Rick turned away and found a long and unburnt plank. He jammed it beneath a broken plank and then tried to lever the door up, but it moved for only a few inches.

After several attempts he noted that the wood flexed in parts, but not at one end, meaning there was probably a catch. If that were so the door had been bolted from below.

'That's not moving,' Todd said at his shoulder, having sneaked up on him.

Rick exhaled sharply. Then, with an exasperated sigh, he held the plank out.

Todd ignored the plank and stomped around the edges of the door. Then he jumped high and slammed his heels down on a corner, which splintered, unbalancing him.

He stumbled backwards and landed on his rump in a heap of wood. Then he leapt to his feet, batting at his pants to remove the hot embers.

For once Rick didn't pour scorn on him, as he'd broken through the wood. He dropped to his knees and used the plank to lever up the remnants of the door. Then he peered down into the exposed space, from where a breeze emerged, giving him the impression of a large space.

As his eyes became accustomed to the lower light level in the hole, he saw steps. These steps put him in mind of the steps down into the cavern beneath the law office.

He sat on the edge of the hole and then jumped several steps down. The area below was dark, but he could see a crate twenty feet away as well as the broad extent of a space that was about fifty feet across and which stretched beyond the back of the building.

While Todd peered into the hole without interest, Rick narrowed his eyes. Then, when he read the writing on the side of the crate, his heart thudded with alarm. He grabbed Todd's arm and pointed to the road.

'Stand guard and make sure nobody gets close,' he said. 'If this is as dangerous as I reckon it is, go and warn Hannibal.'

'Sure,' Todd murmured. Then he sloped off into the road, seemingly content to have been given a task that required him to stand still.

Rick made his way down into the cavern. He had yet to reach the bottom when he confirmed he'd been correct.

The crate was four feet long and two feet high, and stencilled on the side was a legend that claimed it contained dynamite.

CHAPTER 8

Standing in a patch of light coming down from above, Rick considered the crate. He flexed his fingers to loosen up the stress in his muscles and then knelt.

Moving slowly, as if that would somehow reduce the chances of an explosion, he gripped the lid and tugged tentatively. To his relief the lid moved. Holding his breath, he swung it away.

As shadows filled the bottom of the crate he craned his neck. Still he couldn't see anything inside. He lowered his hand into the crate.

He touched something wet and, despite his determination not to make sudden moves, he jerked his hand away. When his heightened senses told him that he had touched only damp wood, he shook his head, chiding himself.

More confident now, he put his hand back in and felt the damp bottom of the crate. Then he inched his fingers from side to side, finding the corners without encountering obstructions. Only then did he tip the crate up to the light and, with relief, he confirmed his expectations.

The crate was empty.

The acrid stench suggested that the warning on the side that the crate contained dynamite had once been correct, but no longer.

While putting his mind to the question of why such a box had been lying beneath Carl's saloon, possibly for some time, Rick explored the extremities of the cavern.

A cooling breeze coming from the furthest, darkest corner rustled his hair. With his eyes narrowed to peer into the gloom, he shuffled forward with his arms stretched out, presuming he was approaching one of the tunnels on Todd's map.

When he was closer to the corner, the breeze became stronger, making him feel that space was ahead, but without light he wouldn't be able to explore it. Since dynamite had once been stored down here, he didn't want to bring down a lamp.

Footfalls clumped on the steps, making him turn, but he'd moved some distance away from the entrance and he couldn't see the person who was coming down.

'Todd,' he called, 'stay up there. I'm coming out.'

The footfalls continued, then a thud sounded as the person leapt down to the floor. Shaking his head at his nephew's failings, Rick headed back into the main cavern and then came to a sudden halt.

He couldn't see anyone. He peered at the steps and then at the crate, the only places where whoever had come down could be lurking.

A crunch sounded behind him a moment before two bunched hands slammed down on the back of his neck, knocking him forward. He went sprawling onto his chest. He tried to raise himself but his hands slipped on the damp rock.

Then his assailant was on him. A second blow hammered down on the back of Rick's head, thudding his forehead into the rock. The blow numbed him and he reckoned he must have passed out as, when he next tried to move, he was on his back and he was being dragged backwards by the legs.

He struggled, but he couldn't find purchase on the rock. So he conserved his strength and looked up, seeing a blurred and swirling view of the cavern roof. He blinked several times, and when his vision focused the steps were further away.

He realized with a start that he was being dragged away from the cavern and down the tunnel. He focused on his attacker and, as he now assumed that the man would be an associate of Hedley Beecher, he recognized him as being Hedley's most trusted man: Jacob Gould.

He didn't waste any time wondering how Jacob had sneaked past his idiotic nephew.

It became darker and colder. The wind that he'd noticed earlier became stronger and Jacob's footfalls echoed.

With a stomp of his feet, Jacob stopped and slapped hands down onto Rick's chest. He drew him up to a sitting position, then swung him round to face absolute darkness.

Rick was still acting docilely while he waited to find out what Jacob had in mind but, when wind lashed his face, with a lurch of his stomach he got the impression that a vast space was before him. Jacob moved behind him, gathered a firm grip of the back of his jacket, and tipped him over to a kneeling position, confirming that he intended to hurl him forward.

Rick heard a roaring sound coming from below. Worried now that the space he sensed ahead also opened up below, he put his hands down on what felt like the lip of a substantial drop, then he pushed upwards.

His sudden movement caught Jacob by surprise and he stumbled away. Heartened, Rick twisted as he came up, but the quick motion made him giddy and he could do nothing other than sway in the dark with his arms outstretched.

His right hand brushed Jacob's chest, but that only gave his opponent the opportunity to grab his wrist and swing him round. In a moment Jacob was behind him. Then he delivered a firm shove to Rick's back while releasing his wrist.

Rick teetered, Jacob's actions confirming that he was on the lip of a large drop and that taking even a short pace forward would make him fall. But he couldn't keep his balance and he toppled.

He just had enough time for a flailing wave of his arms and this time his frantic lunge slapped Jacob's chest. He grabbed hold of his jacket and that stilled his motion with his body angled forward.

Jacob grunted and battered at his arm, trying to dislodge him, but Rick had gathered a tight grip. Then, inexorably as Rick's weight dragged them both down, Rick leaned further forward while behind him Jacob pressed against his back.

Rick moved his feet, trying to find solid ground, but that only speeded his descent. Then, in a rush, he tipped over the side. A scream rent the air and, in his disorientated state, he couldn't tell if he or Jacob had made the noise.

He fell with the rushing air tearing at his face for seemingly ages although it must have been for just a few seconds. Then coldness hammered against his body.

A moment later his befuddled senses told him the coldness was water. But by then he'd gone deep beneath the surface.

The thought came to him that Edison had promised him a trial by water, but by then his lungs demanded air and, in the darkness, he couldn't tell which way was up.

A new and deeper darkness overcame him. The urge to struggle faded. He opened his mouth. Cold water rushed in.

*

'You have to come with me,' Norton Wells demanded, 'now!'

Virginia stared at him around the side of the door to her room with her night robe clutched to her throat.

'It's late and I'm tired. You'll have to wait until. . . .' She trailed off when her gaze took in his full form and she backed away. 'What happened to you?'

Norton fingered a bruise on his cheek. 'Hedley Beecher came for me, but I survived.'

She winced, then beckoned him in, but she didn't close the door after him.

'You're a brave man.' She lowered her voice. 'I knew I could depend on you.'

She gave him a warming smile and the elation that had overcome him on the way back to his mercantile but which had deserted him after his subsequent experience, returned, making him laugh. Even the insistent pain that had hurt with every movement no longer troubled him.

'You've always been able to trust me. So you have to trust me again and leave.'

She'd been nodding, but the last word made her shake her head.

'I told you. Tonight was a reward for agreeing to become my new trusted confidant. Later, I'll set you a task to prove your loyalty and then—'

'I didn't mean I want to take you away from New Town.' He gulped, hoping she hadn't detected the catch in his voice that showed this was what he wanted her to do, one day. 'I meant with Hedley Beecher in town, your life is in danger and you have to stay with me.'

Virginia sighed, then shooed him away.

'I've hired Logan Reed to protect me.' She softened her tone. 'He has his talents and you have yours. I'll use you both, but I'll reserve the special rewards for you alone.'

'When I was with the doctor, I heard he's gone.'

Her eyes narrowed and darkened before she replaced the expression with an encouraging one.

'He'll be doing what he does best.'

Her voice shook and so, with his confidence rising, he took her arm. She squirmed and tried to shake him off, but Norton moved on to the door. She even called out to Jasper for help, but he didn't emerge from his room.

It was only when Norton had reached the end of the corridor that he registered that she was still wearing her night robe. He'd gathered all his resolve to come this far and he reckoned that if he let her get dressed doubts would assail him. He marched on down the stairs with her digging in her heels behind him.

The saloon was closed for the night, so he went through the back door he'd broken down to get inside. Outside, the rain had stopped, but a chill wind had got up, which encouraged her to stop fighting him.

She gave him a long look and, when he released her, she wrapped her robe tightly about her chest and legs. Then they scurried along the backs of the buildings on the main drag to reach the law office.

On the way Norton saw nobody, for which he was thankful as, in his jumpy mood, he reckoned he could start a fight with his own shadow. When they reached the law office, Todd was sleeping in a corner and Hannibal was sitting by the window with his leg propped up on another chair.

'Why are you here?' Hannibal said, eyeing them with bemusement.

'Hedley Beecher,' Norton said.

He drew a Peacemaker from his pocket, something nobody would ever have seen him wield before. Then, as if that was the only explanation he needed, he directed Virginia to sit at the back of the office while he stood beside the door.

With his gaze set on the main drag and the gun resting against his shoulder, he waited for Hedley to come.

CHAPTER 9

Rick's head broke free of the water and he drew in a gasp of air before he again went under.

Over the last few minutes he'd heaved his way to the surface several times. Despite the impenetrable darkness, that small success had let him work out that the water was moving rapidly through an underground passage.

Twice he'd swum as high as he could and he'd knocked against rock, showing that there wasn't always an air space above. He didn't know when he'd next be able to breathe.

He had no choice but to keep fighting to stay afloat and hope he could reach the outlet of the underground river in Hollow Cavern, even though that was at least a mile away. He pushed himself upwards and this time, when he gained the surface he was able to tread water and keep his head in fresh air.

He shook the water from his ears and heard

roaring, the sound seeming to come from all directions. Without any real hope of getting help, he called out and, amidst the cacophony, he heard his voice echoing.

He called again, but this time he heard nothing. When the roaring of the water grew in intensity and gave him the sense that he was about to enter a tunnel again, he dived down.

The current became stronger, seeming to confirm that his guess had been correct. He swam down further and, for the first time since before his plunge, he saw movement ahead. It was faint and he quickly realized he was seeing his own arms.

Encouraged by this observation he fought his way upwards but, to his disappointment, when he broke free of the water he hadn't emerged into the open. But a faint glow was high above and to his right.

This gave him the most hope he'd had so far. He swam towards the glow and, on the third stroke, his leading hand slammed against rock. He cried out, more from shock than pain as the cold water had numbed his limbs.

Then he swam forward again to press his chest against the rock.

In this open area, the current wasn't as strong as earlier and he managed to jam his fingers into a ledge and still himself. With his left hand he sought a higher handhold.

A hand slapped down on his wrist.

Rick screeched and batted the hand away.

'It's me,' a man said from above. It took Rick several moments to place the voice as Logan's.

'Then stop standing around,' Rick shouted, 'and pull me out.'

Two hands wrapped around his left wrist and tugged. With Rick helping his rescuer by scrabbling his feet against the rock, he emerged from the water to land on a ledge two feet above the water level.

Rick sat up and hugged his legs to his chest as he fought to stop himself shivering. He failed, so to distract himself he peered into the darkness until he saw Logan's faint form.

'I thought barring the trapdoor would stop anyone from coming down,' Logan said, 'but I guess you made the same mistake as I did, of exploring after finding the dynamite box.'

'I had more sense than to do that,' Rick said with a light tone that made Logan laugh. 'But I met someone who knew the area better than I did. Jacob Gould threw me into the water. I don't know if he joined me.'

'I've seen only you, but I've only just started to see again, and then not clearly.' Logan took Rick's arm and directed him to look up at the glow. 'I'd guess the moon's broken through the clouds and light is filtering in from somewhere up there.'

Rick patted the area around him to ensure he didn't slip back into the water before he got to his feet.

'Then while we have light, we need to find a way

out of here.'

Logan didn't get up. 'I've already searched. There isn't one.'

Rick still moved away from the water carefully until he reached the end of the cavern. Here the glowing area was above his head and it wasn't as bright as before, suggesting that the illumination was above a ledge.

With his back to the wall and facing the water, he could discern the walls, but only high up. Worse, like the space beneath the Lucky Star and the jailhouse, this cavern had a base that was larger at the bottom than at the top.

Resigned now to accepting that they couldn't climb up walls that sloped inwards, he made his careful way back to Logan.

'No, there isn't a way,' he said simply. 'But Deputy Snyder knows I went through the trapdoor. So I guess we either wait for him to figure out I'm trapped down here, or we shout for help.'

Logan slapped him on the back before throwing back his head.

'Help!' he shouted. Rick joined him and they yelled at regular intervals while they paced back and forth trying to warm up.

By the time Rick's voice had become hoarse, he reckoned his clothes were drier and he'd worked out that the river left the cavern through another tunnel. But the light level was so poor he could see only ripples on the surface.

'There's another option,' he said. 'This water must flow into Hollow Creek and that's a mile out of town. We could jump in the water and let the current take us there.'

'I'd decided that was my last option.' Rick was on the far side of the cavern and he moved towards Logan. 'We don't know how much of the way has air space.'

Rick thought back to his journey here and then considered how fast he reckoned the water moved.

'You're right. There's been a lot of rain recently and that'll have swelled the water. If it's a tunnel all the way, we'll drown.'

Logan started to reply, but he broke off to curse. Then a thud sounded as he lost his footing and fell. Rick didn't react as he'd already stumbled several times, but then Logan whistled through his teeth.

'Come here,' he said. 'I've found something.'

Rick shuffled closer and found that Logan was kneeling. Logan took his hands and guided them towards an object on the ground. When Rick touched Logan's discovery, he also whistled.

Several large bags were sitting in a pile. They were heavy and filled with objects that rattled. The bags were tied up with thick cord and in the dark Rick struggled with the knot. Logan opened a bag first and emptied a handful of the contents onto Rick's palm.

'Coins,' Rick said, 'and lots of them.'

'A fortune if they're silver or gold.'

The coins were cool to the touch, so they felt more like silver than gold. Both men held the coins up to the available light, but as it wasn't bright enough to confirm one thing or the other they both pocketed a handful.

'Last year Hedley Beecher stole ten thousand dollars in silver. Everyone thought the money was long gone, but perhaps it never went anywhere,' said Rick.

'I'd guess that Edison used his knowledge of the tunnels to store dynamite for the raid and then to hide the silver,' opined Logan.

Rick nodded. 'Edison told me a wild tale about me facing trials of air, fire, water and earth tonight. At the time I thought he was taunting me, but now I reckon he'd worked out I'd investigate and find these underground passages.'

Logan sighed as he kicked each bag in turn, confirming that there were five.

'If he knew about the money, Norton Wells could know about it too. And Carl Schmidt appeared to know something.'

'All men who were at the poker game last month.'

Logan slapped a fist into a palm. 'And after that poker game, my brother was shot up.'

Rick fingered a coin, feeling that an understanding of the situation was now dangling tantalizingly close.

'Was he the kind of man who would have worked out that Edison was up to something?'

'Yeah,' Logan murmured, 'which might explain why he left your sister's bed that night, because she sure doesn't know why.'

His tone sounded distracted, presumably as he too was thinking rapidly about what this discovery meant, but it cheered Rick. For the first time he had uncovered a reason why Ogden might have been killed that didn't involve his sister.

He started to ask Logan what else Virginia had told him, but then his teeth started chattering and an unbidden shiver shook his shoulders. That made Logan shiver too.

Exploring the cavern and then piecing together what had been happening recently had taken his mind off how cold he was, but it was now well past midnight and a strong chill was descending.

Rick jumped on the spot and slapped his hands against his arms.

'We may be close to working this out,' he said when his teeth had stopped chattering, 'but if we don't get out of here soon, we'll never get a chance to do anything about it.'

'As you said,' Logan said in a resigned tone, 'we have two choices: either we wait for your idiot nephew to raise the alarm, or we get ourselves out.'

Rick snorted ruefully and turned to the water.

'Come on,' he said, 'before I start thinking about how bad an idea this is.'

They shuffled forward to stand beside the underground river. They both took deep breaths. Then, on the count of three, they jumped in.

Rick had hoped he'd never have to brave the dark terror of the water again, but even so he'd forgotten how strong and unforgiving the current was.

Within seconds he lost a sense of where Logan was, and the dark mass of the rock wall loomed above him.

He dived down and started counting so he could break the surface in a controlled manner. While swimming with the current he kept his hands in front of him to buffer against any knocks, and counted to fifty.

Then he drove upwards. He broke the surface and breathed in deeply, but the area was in complete darkness; he didn't dare stay on the surface for fear that the strong current would make him bang his head on an unseen obstacle.

He dived, stayed down for a count of fifty, then swam back up.

He again broke the surface and, heartened by his success, he repeated the action eight more times. Each time he called out to Logan, but he heard nothing other than the roaring water.

The next time he sought the surface, his hands slapped against rock before the current dragged him away.

His lungs demanded air and he tried again, and then again, but both times he suffered the same result. In the darkness and with no way of telling how far he would have to travel, his heart thudded with panic and he flapped around wildly in the water.

One of his lunges let him grip rock; he held on and stopped moving. Then he drew himself up to press his face to his hands.

Air slipped into his mouth, and gratefully he drew in a long breath; he also drew in water, making him splutter. He closed his mouth and took stock of the situation.

He decided that he'd found a pocket of air, so he pressed his arms up against the rock and put his face behind them. His mouth being sheltered, he could breathe more readily, but the grip he'd gathered wasn't strong and he patted around to find a wider ledge.

His hand closed on something that was cold and clammy, making him recoil until he realized he'd touched skin.

'Logan?' he said, shuffling closer.

A solid blow clumped against his shoulder and then a second wilder blow clipped his forehead.

'It's me,' Rick persisted, raising his voice, but another punch came, this time cracking into his jaw and knocking his forehead against the roof.

Wincing as he moved away, Rick decided he'd found Jacob Gould. He must have fallen into the water after all, and while he and Logan had explored the cavern, he'd been hanging on here.

The thought came that being in the cold for so long would have weakened him. Heartened, Rick stopped moving away and clambered back towards his assailant.

For his trouble he received another wild blow to the chin, but he kept moving until he reached the wide ledge that Jacob was holding on to. Then he bunched a fist and aimed a straight-armed jab at where he reckoned Jacob's face would be.

His fist connected with skin and something that was hard enough to feel like a chin, so he delivered two more quick jabs, only drawing back his fist for a few inches each time.

With the third blow a cry of pain sounded and Jacob tried to batter away his hand, but his action only let Rick orient himself.

He reached under Jacob's head. Then he shoved upwards. He couldn't deliver much force behind the push, but it was strong enough to drive Jacob's face up into the rock ceiling.

Rick flexed his arm, then moved to repeat the action, but he couldn't find Jacob's head. He'd just accepted that he must have dislodged him when a hand gripped his ankle and then attempted to claw its way higher.

Rick settled himself and raised his free leg. Then he kicked down. His boot connected with something solid and the hand slipped down to his foot and then away.

Now feeling as if he'd been left alone, he let the current drive his legs upwards; he hung on with his nose pressed against the rock and his body dangling downstream. As he could breathe, he worked his way underneath the rock, the strong current making him feel as if he were lowering himself downwards.

He moved himself twenty times while keeping his face out of the water, but he felt as if he'd travelled for only a few yards and the cold was cramping his biceps. Then a painful muscle-spasm shot down his forearm and loosened his grip.

He went hurtling off down the river again, his uncontrolled movement banging him into the tunnel roof and then sending him deep under water. He hadn't gathered his breath before going under, so, using his legs, he fought his way back upwards.

To his surprise he emerged out of the water to be confronted with stars and a low moon. He stared at the dazzling moon and cried out with relief.

Before the cold could cramp his limbs again he pushed towards the side, gaining the soft mud at the riverbank in a few strokes. He slithered across the muddy ground until he was free of the water, then got onto his knees and then his feet.

Feeling as if each step would be the only one he could manage, he stomped along for a few paces. He saw that he'd drifted along for fifty yards beyond Hollow Cavern, but getting there to shelter from the chill wind looked like being an epic trek.

His strength faded: he dropped to his knees and then onto his side.

He curled up, trying to generate a warm centre in his body, but his limbs felt like ice and he was sure the effort was futile.

'You have to get up,' Logan said, coming into view. He knelt beside Rick. 'You were gone for so long I thought you'd drowned.'

'I found a place to rest up,' Rick said, through short gasps and chattering teeth. 'I wasn't to know I was only a few yards from the outlet.'

Logan gave him an encouraging pat on the back. Then he drew him up to his feet. Rick wasn't able to help him, but once Logan had got him moving he walked with stronger paces.

The cold wind flattened his drenched clothing against his body, keeping Rick's spirits down and confirming that they needed to get back to town quickly so they could get warm.

'Drenched,' Logan muttered.

When Rick glanced at him he saw that he had meant his gun, which he was wiping on an equally damp jacket sleeve.

'I'd worry about the rest of you being wet first,' Rick said.

'Nope.' Logan turned to town. 'Sunup isn't for a while yet, and long before then I'll need it.'

Rick was about to offer his support, but then the faint sounds of gunfire erupted. The noise was distant and coming from town.

He sighed. Then with Logan he trudged on back to New Town.

CHAPTER 10

Hedley's men were moving around outside and taking up positions closer to the law office.

The clock on the wall said it was approaching two in the morning. Norton reckoned the trouble he'd been expecting for the last hour was about to erupt.

To Norton's way of thinking they'd waited too long. The excitement of dragging Virginia down to the law office and taking control of the situation had now receded, leaving him feeling every cut and bruise from Hedley's beating.

Every time he moved position another dull ache announced itself. He no longer reckoned he had the strength to see off a prolonged siege, and the others wouldn't be much use.

Virginia was sitting at the back of the office, huddled up in her robe beside the sleeping Todd, while Marshal Hannibal had turned to the whiskey to numb the pain in his leg.

Norton wished he'd joined him in drinking liquor,

but it was too late now. Through the window set into the door he saw two men scurry across the road to take up a position out of his view.

'Trouble?' Hannibal asked.

'Yeah,' Norton said. 'Hedley's coming.'

Hannibal downed his whiskey, then levered himself to his feet. He hopped across the office, dragging his chair behind him, and sat beside the left-hand window, from where he could see towards the bulk of town.

Norton pointed out where the men had gone to ground. As Hannibal grunted that he understood footfalls sounded behind him. Norton directed Todd to stand beside the right-hand window.

To his surprise, when he turned he saw that Virginia had come over. She'd claimed her son's Peacemaker, which she was hefting on her palm, appraising its weight.

'That's too powerful for you,' Hannibal said.

'I hope,' she said, 'that when Hedley comes he'll make the same mistake.'

Hannibal laughed, suggesting they'd alluded to a past incident, but their ready familiarity made Norton frown. He pointed at Todd.

'What kind of man lets his mother fight for her life while he sleeps?'

'You've recently become important to me,' Virginia said with coldness in her eyes, 'but don't judge my son or me. Men who do that regret it.'

Norton knew he should back down but, his heart

thudding so hard it drove away his aches and numbness, he moved a pace closer to her.

'Did Ogden Reed judge you?'

'Don't pretend you've worked something out, Norton. You suspect things, but you know nothing.' She sighed. 'That's why I like you. You're more restful company than the men who usually fill my days.'

Norton opened and closed his mouth soundlessly, unsure if he'd been insulted or complimented. He'd yet to decide when a gunshot blasted outside. Then the window to his left shattered.

Two quick shots followed. Norton leapt at Virginia, putting himself between her and the window. Then, with his arms spread, he tried to push her to the floor, but she neatly side-stepped around him and hurried across the open window to kneel beside Marshal Hannibal.

She and Hannibal exchanged amused glances, as if this was something they'd done before. Then Hannibal peered through the broken pane and picked out a target. He loosed off two quick shots, but she stayed her fire.

Norton decided to trust that they knew what they were doing. He knelt down beside the other end of the broken window. Shadows were flitting through the night and although he couldn't discern their forms he blasted lead three times, splaying his gunshots across the stables opposite.

The action cheered him and the shadows stopped

moving. He still blasted another two shots and even shouted with defiance. As he reloaded, Virginia gave him a supportive nod and Hannibal smiled.

'Everyone fine?' Hannibal asked in an assured tone that Norton hadn't heard for a while.

'Sure,' Virginia and Norton said together.

Then they both looked to the back of the law office where Todd was shuffling towards them, stretching his limbs. He pointed at the broken window in a casual manner.

'How did that happen?' he asked around a wide yawn.

After the burst of gunfire that had rattled away in the distance, for the next ten minutes no more gunfire sounded. That was fine with Rick, as he and Logan were in no state to do anything about it.

For the last five minutes, as they'd trudged away from the river, Rick had shivered continuously. Now he felt as if he'd turned into a block of ice. Logan was no longer shivering and Rick reckoned that that meant he was in a worst condition than he himself was.

They shuffled along with their arms wrapped around the other's shoulders, trying to support each other. Despite this, one or both of them stumbled over every other step.

'We have to go back and shelter in Hollow Cavern,' Logan said.

'No,' Rick said, his jaw aching from the effort of

talking. 'We have to keep going. If we stop, we'll never move again.'

'Sounds good,' Logan murmured. He stomped to a halt.

Rick gathered a firm grip of his arm and he tried to drag him on, but Logan pointed over his shoulder at the dark mass of the cavern and then shuffled round to face it. He moved on for a pace.

'We don't need shelter.' Rick dragged Logan back. 'The sky's clear now, so it'll just get colder. We need warmth, and we can only get that in town.'

It took all of his willpower to utter these words. Then he could no longer make his hand hold its grip on Logan and he lowered his arm. Then his legs gave way and he dropped, swaying, to his knees.

'Look,' Logan murmured. For several seconds he pointed at the cavern, but then his strength gave out too and his arm flopped down to rest on Rick's shoulder.

Rick couldn't muster the energy to seek out what had caught Logan's interest and he did not argue when, with a grunt of effort, Logan dragged him to his feet and set off back towards the cavern with a stumbling gait.

Every pace jolted Rick's body and his feet felt like wooden blocks, but Logan had gathered a burst of strength, so he let him walk him on.

As they approached the water he listened to the thundering of the river, but that only made him feel colder. To comfort himself, and to take his mind off the cold, he counted paces.

When he reached thirty his mind wouldn't tell him what the next number was. For some reason this number felt important.

So he concentrated on working it out while he restarted his counting from one. He had reached a new stumbling block of twenty when his slow thoughts told him that a more important matter than the number was ahead: a light.

It was just a dull glow, perhaps from a guarded campfire that they hadn't noticed from down by the water's edge. Rick reckoned that anyone who had holed up outside town on a bitterly cold night would probably not welcome an intrusion, but a bad reaction was better than dying from the cold and he forced himself to speed up.

With him now helping Logan, they broke into a shuffling run. The glow burned itself into Rick's vision and he willed it to be within reach after the next step, and then after the next, but it remained beyond his grasp.

Then the rhythm of their footfalls changed and they both stumbled. Rick hit the hard ground, where he rolled over to lie on his back staring upwards.

Even the stars were no longer shining down on him and he saw only utter darkness.

Accepting he'd reached the end, he closed his eyes. He counted his heartbeats, but this time he couldn't remember what number came after eight.

He started again and this time he could reach only

three. Then, seemingly a great distance away, he heard Logan stomping around.

Hands slapped down on his shoulders and dragged him along. Weakly he tried to push the hands away, but he failed to stop his tormentor from tugging him. He opened his eyes, meaning to implore him to leave him alone.

It was lighter than before and, with hope fluttering in his guts, he craned his neck. Five feet away a fire was crackling.

'Heat,' Rick murmured as, with a supreme effort, he rolled over onto his knees. He crawled towards the flames.

'The fire was almost out,' Logan said, 'but I got it going again.'

Logan hurried round to the other side of the fire and stood over the flames. Rick followed him at a lower level, not caring how close he got to the flames as he breathed in the delicious smoke.

'Anyone else here?' Rick asked after he'd enjoyed the warmth for a while.

Logan sat down and started wringing out water from his jacket.

'Whoever was here has gone.'

Rick looked around and, with a smile, he noted why the stars were no longer visible. They were in a cave.

As the light from the fire barely reached the walls and roof, they were in Hollow Cavern. This was where last year Jasper had crippled himself and where last month Marshal Hannibal had broken his leg.

'People don't usually spend the night here,' Rick said. He winced as his slow thought process pieced together the situation. 'But Hedley Beecher and his gunslingers have. They appeared in town without horses several days after the train passed through, and like Edison last month they disappeared quickly.'

Logan nodded. He paused in his attempts to dry himself to root around in his pocket. He drew out a handful of coins that reflected the light dully. When Rick examined the coins he'd pocketed, he was sure they were silver.

Logan continued to search his pockets until he slapped the ground in irritation.

'I lost the map in the water,' he said. 'Without it, we'll never work out how to get back to the silver.'

Rick pocketed his coins and warmed his hands, his spirits rising.

'That's no problem,' he said. 'I know where we can get another copy.'

CHAPTER 11

Despite the earlier gunfire, New Town was quiet, but Rick and Logan still approached the first buildings on the edge of town stealthily.

They'd heard no gunfire since they'd found the fire over an hour ago. Having used that time to dry off and get warm, they were both in better spirits than they had been when they'd taken refuge in Hollow Cavern.

'The law office window's broken,' Logan said, craning his neck as he peered ahead.

Rick side-stepped to stand beside the stables, from where he confirmed Logan's observation. A light burned in the office, suggesting that Hedley hadn't freed Edison yet.

Logan joined him and they both edged along the wall to get a better view of the office.

'If Hedley laid siege to the office,' Rick whispered,

'he didn't get far.'

'With only Hannibal and your idiot nephew to get past,' Logan said, 'he should have succeeded, unless the coins are his target and not Edison.'

Logan moved on, walking less cautiously than before. Rick stayed several steps behind him and, when Logan came to a sudden halt and levelled his gun on the alley beside the law office, he darted into the shadows.

A moment later Hedley Beecher looked around the corner of the office. Hedley glanced along the boardwalk, then gestured with his gun to two men in the shadows. The three men slipped around the corner and made their cautious way to the window.

If they looked across the road, Logan would be in clear view, but the men were intent on getting closer to the window. Then, perhaps because Hedley had been heard inside the office, Rick saw someone hurry past the broken window and then duck down to the side.

He couldn't be sure, but it had appeared to be a woman. He peered at the window, but before he saw her again Hedley pressed his back to the wall and looked across the road.

Hedley flinched, clearly being uncertain as to whether he should move on or go back. Then he raised his gun, and in response Logan crouched down while levelling his own six-shooter on him.

Logan fired and his gunshot kicked dust from the wall a foot above Hedley's head. Hedley went to one knee and returned gunfire that sliced into the dirt several feet in front of Logan, giving Logan enough time for a second shot and for Rick to join him in shooting.

Both their shots pounded into the wall, one slug landing so close to Hedley's head that it made him drop down further, while the other shot made one of his men feel his shoulder, as if he'd been nicked.

Hedley glanced at both his men and gave them a quick overhead gesture. Then, while firing so rapidly that they forced Logan and Rick to duck down, they headed back to the alley.

Rick and Logan closed ranks. They trained their guns on the corner as they waited for Hedley to risk coming out again, but when a long minute had passed without him showing himself, Logan set off across the road, closely followed by Rick.

'It's Deputy Cody,' Rick shouted as they ran past the office window. Inside the office several people bobbed up into view before slipping away.

Logan showed no such caution and he ran on past the window, only pausing when he reached the corner. Rick took a wider path so that he could see down the alley: he glimpsed the three men before they scooted away behind the adjoining building.

'There's just the three of them,' Marshal Hannibal shouted from inside the office, raising himself into view behind the window.

Rick nodded, then he and Logan gave chase. They hurried down the dark alley, stopping to listen only

106

when they reached the end. Rapid footfalls were receding, so they moved on around the corner.

The three men were twenty yards ahead, moving with their heads down, seeking shadows. But the lowering moon meant Rick could see them clearly. Logan raised his gun, but instead of firing he glanced at Rick; Rick shook his head.

'We need to find out where they're going,' he said.

Logan firmed his jaw, appearing as if he'd ignore his suggestion. Then, with a grunt of support, he set off after the men with Rick at his side.

They followed them past several buildings until they reached the back of Norton's mercantile. Then the three men ducked into an alley that would take them back to the main drag.

Logan blasted off a quick shot, presumably in irritation. Then he put on a burst of speed. He had opened up a lead of several paces by the time he reached the mercantile.

Without slowing, he swung around the corner, displaying caution only by going in low. He fired high while crouching, then threw himself to the ground and rolled into the shadows.

Rick followed him but stopped at the corner and knelt. Then he slipped round the corner with his head down and lay on his chest.

He could see a slither of the road at the other end of the alley. The fleeing men shouldn't have reached the road by now, but he couldn't see their forms and he was lying with his face only inches from the ground.

He rocked from side to side, but he could see nothing other than the dark alley walls. Logan shuffled sideways to join him.

'Hedley must have found a door,' Logan whispered.

'There isn't one,' Rick said, summoning up an image of the alley during daylight.

Logan nodded. 'In that case you take one side of the alley. I'll take the other.'

Rick stood and pressed his back to the wall. Then, walking sideways, he edged along the wall with his gun drawn and held low in his right hand, his left hand feeling the wall ahead.

He kept pace with Logan, who adopted his cautious approach, but they didn't come across the men and, when the light level grew, he accepted they weren't here. Logan became agitated as he clearly came to the same conclusion, and he ran to the end of the alley.

His hands on his hips, Logan looked up and down the road, then shook his head. The two men made their way back while craning their necks, but it seemed that Hedley had again disappeared and the implications made Rick smile.

'The underground cavern is somewhere below us,' he said, pointing downwards. 'As light got down to us, Hedley can get down too.'

'It's a pity,' Logan said, 'that the rain will have washed away the copy of the map you used.'

Rick smiled. 'It will have, but we can hope that it won't have washed away the only sensible thing my nephew's ever done.'

Logan cast him a doubtful look, but neither man spoke again as they walked back to the law office. They were cautious and, when they reached the broken window, they both peered down the main drag.

Nobody was about other than, to Rick's surprise, Norton Wells, who was loitering in the doorway. He tensed when he saw them and then beckoned them in.

He stood hunched with an arm held across his chest. His eyes were bright with what Rick took to be either fever or liquor.

'Get in,' Norton said, talking quickly while gesturing, 'before Hedley comes back. I've been fighting him off all night, but he wasn't ornery enough to get past me.'

Rick reckoned that any man whom Norton had fought off wouldn't be formidable, but he kept that thought to himself and slipped inside.

He got a second surprise when he found his sister standing by the door; the Peacemaker she'd tucked into the belt of her robe suggested that if anyone had fought off Hedley, it would have been her.

Marshal Hannibal was sitting by the window with his leg raised on a chair. A half-empty whiskey bottle on the floor showed how he was keeping the pain at bay. Todd was skulking around at the back of the office in his usual bored manner.

Virginia greeted him with a warm smile. Rick led her away from the others.

'We found something interesting,' he whispered, keeping his voice low so that only she could hear. 'It might explain why Ogden was killed.'

'What is it?' she whispered, her wide eyes appearing keenly interested and not looking as if she'd already guessed their discovery.

'Later and not here,' Rick said, glancing at the others to show the reason for his silence.

She nodded. 'If Hedley doesn't make a move in the next few minutes, I'm going back to the saloon.'

Rick wondered if he should discourage her plan, but Norton called from the doorway.

'I can't protect you out there,' he said.

Virginia gave Rick an exasperated look. Then she returned to the others while he joined Todd at the back of the office.

'I did as you ordered and came here,' Todd said with a bowed head. 'Norton brought my mother along.'

'I'm not blaming you,' Rick said, keeping to himself the thought that he might have followed orders, but he hadn't shown initiative. 'I can see you're getting used to this job, so now I need your help. I want you to draw me that map again, this time on paper.'

Todd brightened; without demur, he went to the desk that had previously been Rick's. With a glance at

Hannibal, who wasn't paying them any attention, he removed a folded wanted poster from the bottom drawer and started scribbling on the back.

While he worked Rick stood between him and the people at the front of the office. Logan distracted everyone's attention by quizzing them on what had happened here for the last few hours.

With nobody watching them, from the corner of his eye Rick watched the map take shape and he was impressed with the way Todd drew. He used firm strokes that unerringly marked out the details he'd seen on the sack and, as he was working from a memory of a design he'd seen only once, Rick wondered for the first time if he'd misjudged him.

'You have a talent,' he whispered when Todd pushed the finished map towards him.

'I don't,' Todd grumbled. 'I hate being a deputy.'

Rick didn't want to say too much and risk being overheard, so he answered him with a smile that conveyed he hoped he would find the right path soon. Then he considered the map.

As he now knew that the topmost circle was the cavern beneath the Lucky Star, he was sure that the largest circle, which was at the bottom, was Hollow Cavern. Three circles were between them and their positions made him smile.

He pocketed the map and went to join Logan.

'We'll check to see if Hedley's around,' he said, looking at Virginia. 'Don't go back to the saloon until we return.'

111

'Don't worry.' She winked. 'Norton's looking after me.'

CHAPTER 12

'This doesn't help us,' Logan said, moving Rick's hands aside so that the low moonlight illuminated the map. 'It doesn't show anything above ground.'

'I'd guess,' Rick said, 'the original was mapped out long before New Town came along, but it proves something is beneath us.'

Logan turned away to consider the Lonesome Trail. He had taken an oil lamp from the law office; holding it high he peered through the window.

'You've worked here for two years. You have more hope than I do of finding a way down.'

Rick shrugged. 'I've never come across anything like the trapdoor at the Lucky Star.'

Logan nodded and moved on towards Norton's mercantile, leaving Rick to consider the map. He measured the distance from the Lucky Star to Hollow Cavern, but the scale wasn't precise enough to help him judge where to look.

Then he noticed something he hadn't seen

113

before. Todd had drawn a spur off one of the tunnels, suggesting that a hard-to-find entrance might be close by.

Feeling more confident, he joined Logan as he put a shoulder to the mercantile door. When he'd burst in, Rick stood in the centre of the main room amidst the strewn produce while Logan found a low, hinged hatchway in the wall.

Logan considered him with a triumphant look that made Rick frown, as he hadn't noticed the hatch before. Thinking quickly to get over his irritation, he recalled the last time he'd stood in this room, earlier in the evening.

Hedley had spoken near by. Back then Rick had thought he was outside, but recent events made him look at the counter and then downwards.

He hurried behind the counter and found a mat close to the door in the wall. It lay askew, as if tossed aside, and when he went down on his knees he found a small bolted trapdoor in the floor near by.

Logan raised the trapdoor to find it led down to a cellar where, presumably, Norton moved deliveries from the outside into storage.

The two men exchanged smiles. Logan passed the lamp to Rick and moved from side to side while searching for the best way to jump down. Then he jerked away.

A moment later a gunshot blasted out, the slug cannoning into the roof.

Logan snarled with irritation and drew his gun. He

thrust his arm forward and fired down through the hole without looking. The gunshot was still echoing when he leapt down, to disappear from view.

Rick drew his own gun and, acting more cautiously than Logan had done, he edged closer to the trap-door. Grunting sounded below along with scuffling feet; he jerked his head forward.

When the raised lamp illuminated the cellar he saw what he'd expected to see.

Logan was tussling with one of the men who had been sneaking up on the law office. That meant Hedley and another man would be close by. Rick moved forward while peering around the lit-up section of the cellar.

His foreshortened view of the scene below let him see Logan and his assailant turning on the spot, each man holding the other's gun arm stretched high. He lowered the lamp to banish the shadows, and that presented him with the sight of a man's legs standing in the centre of the cellar.

Rick side-stepped away while crouching; his defensive action encouraged the second man to shoot at him.

The gunshot cannoned into the counter behind him, passing so close that a metallic click sounded and the oil lamp shook in his hand. Rick placed the lamp on the floor and then knelt side-on to the trap-door.

If he edged forward any more the second gunman would be able to see him, but he didn't want to extinguish the light and put Logan at a disadvantage. Then he noticed that the gunman had shot at the lamp, suggesting he'd been in the dark for a while and had been dazzled.

So, before the man got his full vision back, Rick grabbed a nearby sack of corn and dragged it closer. He stood it upright and then pushed, toppling the sack over the side and into the cellar.

The sack drew two rapid gunshots, helping Rick to pinpoint where the gunman was. He swayed forward and picked out his form standing five feet away.

This man was still aiming at the sack, giving Rick enough time to aim carefully. With confidence he slammed a deadly shot into his chest, which dropped him to his knees and then on to his front.

Rick stayed in position and, to his delight, his action had a second effect when Logan's assailant backed into the fallen sack and tripped over it. He fell while trying to drag Logan down with him, but Logan kept his balance. The moment his gun arm came free he fired down at the man's chest.

The man twitched once, then rolled off the sack, coming to a halt propped up against the second man.

'Obliged,' Logan said. He looked around. 'And Hedley's not here.'

Rick passed the oil lamp down.

'So let's see what interested these two.'

When Rick had jumped down, Logan looked behind barrels and crates while Rick explored the area. Logan had more luck: in the far corner he found a hole in the floor, about three feet across, through which a cold wind blew.

Logan got Rick's attention. Then he wasted no time in jumping down through the hole. This movement cut off the light in the cellar and Rick had no choice but to follow him.

They found themselves standing at the end of a low tunnel. They edged forward for a few paces, but then to avoid banging their heads on the roof they had to duck down and walk doubled over.

Rick reckoned they were in the spur; he was proved right when after a few dozen paces they came out into a larger tunnel. To their left and towards the Lonesome Trail the tunnel opened up into a dark space. To the right and towards the law office, the tunnel continued beyond the range of the lamp.

They went to the left and after a few paces Rick heard roaring, the sound growing with every pace until they emerged from the tunnel and came out onto a ledge. They shuffled to the edge and peered over the side.

Rick could see nothing below, but when Logan raised the lamp high, it illuminated a vast cavern.

'This is where we climbed out of the river,' Logan said, pointing at a seam of lighter rock on the wall. 'I remember seeing that.'

Rick considered the seam and then raised his gaze up the wall to a dangling rope that reached halfway to the base and which presumably they hadn't been able to see earlier in the night. When he pointed it out to Logan, they followed it until it disappeared into another tunnel entrance.

This tunnel was twenty feet away from the end of the ledge. The heaps of boulders on the cavern bottom suggested that until recently this ledge had provided a solid base for the tunnel, but a section of the rock had eroded away. Rick looked at the swirling mass of water below.

'The river looks wider than I imagined it when we were down there. The rain must have soaked through and swollen it.'

Logan winced and dropped to his knees. He narrowed his eyes and pointed straight down.

Rick quickly saw what had worried him. The five bags of silver were heaped up and the water was lapping at the pile. He reckoned the underground river had risen by several feet in the last few hours and now it threatened to wash the bags away.

'If Hedley wants to get to the silver,' Logan said, 'he'll have to hurry.'

'So why isn't he down there now?'

'I don't know.' Logan looked back down the tunnel that stretched away in the opposite direction. 'So we'd better find out.'

'How much longer do we have to wait?' Virginia said, glancing through the window.

Norton raised a hand to put it on her shoulder, but then thought better of it while Todd and

Hannibal were in the room.

'We wait until Rick and Logan come back,' he said. 'You heard the shooting.'

'I did, and that's what I'm worried about.'

Norton searched for an appropriate reply, but even though she must be concerned for her brother, he wondered if she might be worried about Logan too. He gripped his gun tightly to stave off a twinge of jealousy.

Virginia must have seen the fight go out of him as she gave him a warm smile. This lifted his spirits, but before he could enjoy the feeling a deep, rumbling thud sounded.

The noise was almost a physical movement that he felt with his body rather than with his ears. Then the floor shook, making Virginia take Todd's hand to keep her balance while Hannibal toppled sideways from his chair.

Norton placed his arms wide apart and steadied himself. Then he grabbed Virginia's shoulders and held her tightly. She didn't complain; instead she murmured soothing words to Todd, who looked around in a confused manner.

Then, as suddenly as the shaking had started, it stopped. Years ago Norton had survived tunnel collapses in the mine; now he bustled Virginia out through the door. Todd gathered enough of his wits to follow.

The moment he'd got her safely out on the hardpan, Norton hurried back into the law office to find Hannibal lying on his side, groaning and clutching his thigh while staring at his splinted lower leg.

'You have to get out,' Norton said, taking his arm. 'If there's another tremor, the building could collapse.'

Hannibal shook him off. 'That was no earthquake, you fool.'

He pointed to the corner of the office where a funnel of dust was rising through the grille over the jailhouse. With a wince, Norton put together what had happened.

'Jailbreak,' he murmured.

'Yeah,' Hannibal said. 'See if Edison's gone.'

Norton scurried into the corner and looked through the grille. Thick dust blocked his vision, but a light was moving around and hushed voices were sounding.

'He's being broken out, right now,' Norton whispered, hurrying back to Hannibal.

'Then stop them!' Hannibal blustered, his anger giving him the strength to sit up.

While Hannibal struggled to get to his feet Norton considered the grille. Then, through the window, he looked at Virginia, who was looking nervously down the main drag towards her saloon.

'I'm no deputy,' he said.

Then he batted his hands together and headed to the door. On the way he ignored Hannibal's complaints and, once outside, he took Virginia's arm.

'Edison's escaping,' he said in a matter-of-fact

manner. 'What do you want to do?'

'Go back to the Lonesome Trail,' Virginia said.

'Then I'll escort you,' he said, and they set off.

They had walked for fifty yards and the saloon had become visible ahead when Norton realized with a start that she hadn't complained about him taking her arm. In fact she was gripping his elbow tightly.

When he looked over his shoulder he saw Todd scurrying after them. And, to his surprise, Marshal Hannibal had dragged himself out of the office.

The marshal stood propped up against the wall. Then, hugging the wall to keep him upright, with an uncertain gait he set off after them.

CHAPTER 13

'You fine?' Logan asked when the echoes from the explosion had subsided.

'Yeah,' Rick said, 'and at least we now know for sure what Hedley wanted. His half-hearted open raid on the law office was just a distraction to stop anyone noticing the real escape attempt.'

Logan nodded and then peered down the darkened tunnel. At the furthest extent that the lamplight could reach, dust was swirling, confirming that the tunnel went towards Edison's cell and that that was where the blast had occurred.

They were around 200 yards from the law office. Since the tunnel walls were smooth and afforded them little protection, they retreated. They stopped when they reached a point halfway back to the hole beneath the mercantile.

Here a rock had fallen away from the tunnel wall. Rick lay on his chest behind the rock while Logan stood in the recess left by the rock. Rick placed the lamp on the ground, guarding most of the light, then lowered the light level to a spluttering flame.

They waited; presently voices sounded ahead. Rick couldn't hear what was being said, but the tone was jubilant. Then a moving light appeared down the tunnel. Dust shrouded the glow, but it was bright enough to light up a line of five men.

They'd spread out across the tunnel with three men walking slightly ahead of the others. After they'd moved on for a dozen paces, Rick saw that Edison was in the centre walking with his head down; two men were flanking him and holding his arms behind his back.

'Edison doesn't look happy,' Logan whispered, 'that he's been broken out of jail.'

'That's because we've got it wrong,' Rick whispered back. 'Hedley's not broken him out for his own good.'

Logan nodded; then, as the line of men was only twenty yards away, both men stayed quiet. Logan levelled his gun on the man to Edison's right, so Rick aimed at the man to Edison's left.

The men moved on, letting Rick see that their leader, Hedley, was behind the first group along with another four men, although they frequently looked backwards in case they were being followed.

Edison was ten yards away when the man nearest their side of the tunnel wall stopped and got the others' attention by pointing at them while drawing his gun.

123

Rick lost no time in firing. Logan reacted at the same time. Two crisp shots rang out from Rick's gun, blasting his target in the chest, while Logan fired once, downing his target with a deadly shot to the head.

In a moment Hedley's men got their wits about them and retaliatory gunfire tore out, forcing Logan to jerk backwards into his recess while Rick hugged the ground.

Rapid footfalls sounded and Rick thought one man was embarking on a reckless assault. He rolled onto his side and aimed upwards, awaiting the moment when the running man became visible, but when Edison ran past he stayed his fire.

Edison didn't even glance their way as he kept his head down and made his bolt for freedom down the tunnel with the sureness of a man who had been in these tunnels before.

Rick looked at Logan and the two men exchanged nods. Then they raised their arms.

Firing blind, they blasted two quick shots apiece down the tunnel before following Edison. Rick took several seconds to gain his feet; he was three paces behind Logan by the time both men had speeded up to a brisk run.

The tunnel veered to the right. They kept close to the wall, seeking any available cover. When Hedley's men got their wits about them and shot at their fleeing forms, slugs whined off the tunnel wall or flew overhead before ricocheting away down the tunnel.

124

Rick glanced over his shoulder to see that the men were giving chase. When he turned back Edison had reached the spur that led up to the mercantile. He slowed to round the corner, but five seconds later he hurried out with his head down.

A gunshot blasted and hammered into the wall behind Edison, making him run past the entrance to the spur. Edison's reaction showed that someone was blocking the way out through the mercantile so Rick shouted a warning to Logan, but Logan had already had the same thought.

Logan thrust his head down and sprinted past the entrance. Rick followed his lead. He moved too quickly to see how many men were there, but he noticed that a light now burned at the other end of the tunnel.

That observation made him wince as he realized he'd left the lamp behind: the only light illuminating the tunnel was coming from behind, so, as he came out onto the ledge, he slowed.

Rick also slowed, but Edison showed no such caution. He sprinted across the ledge at a speed that made Rick reckon he was planning to throw himself off the end.

At the last moment Edison appeared to notice the danger he was in. With a wave of the arms and a frantic double-take that made him fall over, he slid to a halt on his side only two feet from the edge.

He got to his knees and peered down. His mouth fell open in surprise, confirming Rick's earlier observation that the ledge had collapsed only recently.

Edison moved away from the edge and sought another direction in which to flee, but Rick and Logan were blocking his path.

'There's nowhere to run,' Logan said.

'There sure isn't,' Edison said. He looked past them down the tunnel where Hedley's men were pounding closer. 'But then again, I could say the same to you.'

Logan grabbed Edison's jacket in a bunched fist and drew him up close. Edison tensed, but Logan did nothing more than turn him around and march him back towards the tunnel.

On either side of the entrance the ledge spread out for ten feet before tapering off to a crumbling edge. The area was fragile, but Rick and Logan had no choice other than to seek refuge there and hope it'd support their weight.

As Logan manoeuvred Edison to the left of the entrance, Rick took the river side. With his back pressed against the wall beside the tunnel, he listened.

Hedley's men were being silent, so Rick glanced round the corner. Most of the men had sought refuge in the spur while two more were lying down on their chests beside the opposite wall.

They were being vigilant and they snapped their guns towards him, forcing him to back away. He caught Logan's eye on the other side of the tunnel and conveyed their predicament with gestures.

Logan nodded and turned his attention onto Edison. He swung him round to place his back to the wall and raised him up onto tiptoes.

'We're pinned down here,' he muttered, slamming him back against the wall, 'but it'll take Hedley time to get to you, time in which I can make you suffer. So tell me: did you kill my brother Ogden Reed?'

Edison couldn't meet Logan's eye; he looked at Rick, who, as he found his earnest gaze disconcerting, glanced round the corner.

A slug whined from one of their opponents, forcing him to back away. He also noticed that a third man had joined them and they'd all moved a few feet forward.

'I didn't, so question Rick, not me,' Edison said. 'He knows I'm not lying. I predicted what'd happen to him tonight and it all happened, didn't it, Rick?'

'Earlier your predictions made no sense,' Rick said, gesturing at the river below, 'but after we found these tunnels I understood. Events you could later claim were trials by air, water, fire and earth were guaranteed to happen down here.'

'That's no matter. My final prediction still holds true: to avoid the final trial by earth you'll tell the truth.'

'We're all facing the same trial under ground.' Rick paused to listen to Hedley barking orders down the tunnel for his men to move in on them. 'You're as likely to die as we are, seeing as how I don't reckon Hedley was rescuing you.'

Edison flared his eyes in defiance. 'You don't know nothing.'

Edison's taunt made Rick withdraw a silver coin from his pocket. He tossed it in the air, letting the light catch it.

'Is this what Hedley really wants?' Edison sneered, so Rick continued: 'You hid the money down here after you stole it from Hedley. That's what the argument during the poker game was really about: not ten dollars, but ten thousand!'

Edison raised his chin in defiance. 'You're not as clever as you think you are. I followed Hedley's orders and hid the silver, except I didn't tell him where I'd hidden it.'

Rick shrugged, conceding that this wasn't important, giving Logan enough time to speak.

'How does my brother fit into this?' Logan demanded.

Edison took a deep breath. 'I didn't kill him, but he did piece together what I'd done and he tried to steal the silver. As with me, it was more important to him than Rick's sister and the things she wanted him to do for her.'

Edison looked at Rick again and grinned, clearly relishing delivering his accusation. As Rick reckoned it'd sound less damning coming from his lips, he was about to mention his earlier suspicion which, after finding the silver, he no longer thought valid, when

128

he heard scrambling.

He cast a worried glance down the length of tunnel as far as he could see. Nobody was visible although shadows were moving on the tunnel wall.

The shadows closed on the entrance; they must have approached Rick's side too, as Logan pressed himself to the wall, releasing his tight grip of Edison.

Then an order reverberated down the tunnel.

'Take them,' Hedley shouted. 'But I want Edison alive!'

CHAPTER 14

When Norton reached the Lonesome Trail Jasper was downstairs. He kept a second wheelchair at the bottom of the stairs and was dragging himself into it.

'I assume,' he said, 'that that explosion means Edison's escaped.'

'We reckon so,' Norton said.

'Then I'm pleased. This matter should be ended before sunup.'

He removed a six-shooter from his pocket and placed it on his lap. Then he wheeled himself across the room.

As Virginia didn't follow him Norton went to her side and stood in a protective position at the bottom of the stairs. Todd joined him and stared up the stairs longingly until, with a deep sigh, he sat on the bottom step.

Jasper wheeled himself past the bar to the private gaming-room. Norton reckoned it hadn't been used since the ill-fated night of the game with Edison Dent.

At the door, Jasper swung round to consider them; when his gaze rested on Norton he smiled.

'What are you smirking at?' Norton demanded, expecting Jasper to say he was barred from the saloon.

'Since my accident Virginia's had many admirers,' Jasper said, his smile growing. 'I'm pleased she's now turned to you.'

'Why?' Norton snapped, feeling sure that he wasn't being paid a compliment.

'Because it was hard not to be jealous about the others, but seeing the depths she's sunk to makes me realize I'm still above her.'

Jasper flashed Virginia a triumphant look that made her turn away. Then he laughed before he wheeled his way through the door.

'Why did he say that?' Virginia murmured. 'I thought we understood each other.'

She looked at Norton, her imploring gaze requesting answers. Norton stared at her with the blood thundering in his ears now that Jasper had given him a chance to drive a wedge between them.

'He doesn't love you,' he said and, having spoken, the words came easily. 'But I do. You don't need him. I have money, lots of money. We can be together, always.'

She considered him, an enigmatic smile lighting her face. Long moments passed in which Norton's future whirled through his mind, a thrilling life filled with Virginia and all the things he'd never thought a man like him would ever enjoy.

'All right,' she whispered.

'You mean it?' Norton blurted out as the room seemed to sway, making him feel giddier than when the explosion had ripped through the jailhouse.

'I do.' She gripped his shoulder and then brushed his cheek with the back of her hand. 'But first, you have to do one small task for me to prove I can trust you. Then we can be together, for ever.'

Her gaze moved to the gaming-room door. Then she glared at it, her fierce stare hot enough to burn a hole through the wood.

Norton couldn't bring himself to follow her gaze, hoping that he'd misunderstood. He looked over her shoulder at Todd, who was now lying back on the stairs staring at the ceiling in a bored manner.

'Is there any other way?' he murmured.

'I'm selfish, I know.' She turned back to him and fluttered her eyelashes. 'Can you live with that?'

He opened his mouth to ask why she wanted him of all men to do this, but the thought came that surely he wouldn't be the first man she'd asked. If that were the case, the last man to be close to her was Ogden Reed, and he'd been killed in that very gaming-room.

He was still struggling to speak when Marshal Hannibal shuffled through the main door, giving him a welcome distraction. The marshal leaned against the wall with a weary sigh.

'You should have stayed in the law office,' Norton said, his voice emerging as a high-pitched lilt.

'Edison's gone,' Hannibal said between gasps. 'I have to catch him.'

'You're in no state to catch anybody.'

Norton's criticism appeared to give Hannibal renewed strength. With a roll of the shoulders he pushed himself away from the wall and embarked on the short hobbled journey to the bar.

Then he worked his way along the counter until he faced the stairs. He flexed his arms, but Virginia pre-empted his next move by pointing to the gaming-room.

'Jasper's in there,' she said.

Hannibal forced a thin smile. 'The appropriate place to end this.'

His forceful tone and strange answer gave Norton the odd feeling that the marshal had just decided to kill Jasper. He shook off his shock and gripped Virginia's arm.

'I'm the one who'll end this,' he said.

Then he set off purposefully for the room, lengthening his stride as he passed the hobbling marshal. He threw open the door.

He hadn't known what he planned to do when he met Jasper, but he came to a sudden halt in the doorway and his enthusiasm to force a confrontation faded away.

Jasper wasn't here. The door was the only

entrance and, like last month, the poker table and chairs were in the middle of the room. Jasper's wheelchair stood beside a cabinet in which he kept his finest liquor.

After a few moments Hannibal's hand clamped down on his shoulder and the marshal rested against him while he considered the deserted room.

Without showing even a flicker of surprise, the marshal worked his way along the wall to the wheelchair and flopped down into it. He rested his head on the back and heaved a grateful sigh. Then he wheeled the chair away from the wall to reveal an open space beside the cabinet.

'Just like in your cellar,' Hannibal said with a smile.

'How do you know about that?' Norton said.

Hannibal merely returned another amused smile. Then he wheeled the chair into position before the gap, but his offhand manner made Norton snarl. He grabbed the back of the chair and pushed the chair away from the wall.

As the wheels couldn't turn quickly enough, they creaked ominously. After a couple of turns the chair tipped over backwards and deposited Hannibal on the floor.

While Hannibal lay groaning, Norton dropped to his knees and looked through the gap. The space behind the wall was cold and the floor sloped away sharply.

At the limit of his vision, a glow was bobbing

around, which after he'd peered at it for a few moments, he discerned as being Jasper dragging himself onwards while pushing a lamp before him.

Norton reckoned there was enough light for him to catch up with him quickly, but before he could slip through the gap Hannibal's groans drew Virginia and Todd into the room. She glanced at the gap in the wall without surprise while Todd considered Hannibal with his head cocked on one side.

'Be careful,' Virginia said with a warm smile.

As Hannibal floundered on the floor, lost in his own private torment after jarring his leg, Norton felt emboldened enough to wink at her.

'I sure will,' he said. 'I'll come back for you and then we'll be together.'

His determined tone and confident attitude made Virginia grin. Then she backed away through the door. Todd dallied as he appraised Hannibal.

'The marshal broke his leg in Hollow Cavern,' he declared.

Norton didn't have the patience that others had when dealing with Todd, but as Virginia's son would be a part of his new life, he smiled.

'He sure did. So after I've gone, look after him.'

He patted Todd's shoulder and turned away, but Todd hadn't finished.

'My father was found in Hollow Cavern too. He was all broke up.'

Norton stopped with his hand on the top of the gap.

'What are you saying?'

'My uncle said I'm not the idiot everyone reckons I am. That's because I notice things, things that others don't.'

Norton turned to see Todd's eyes gleaming with enthusiasm. He had never seen him with such a lively expression before, but he didn't expect it to last for long, so he spoke quickly.

'Have you noticed something recently that others haven't seen?'

Todd shrugged, his eyes lowering. 'They must have fallen from a height, but you can't climb in Hollow Cavern. So perhaps they fell somewhere else and then they dragged themselves to the cavern.'

He yawned and that statement seemed to end his brief period of being interested in something. He shuffled through the door to join Virginia, who gave him a comforting hug around the shoulders, which he shrugged off.

When Norton saw that Hannibal had got over his distress and was sitting up, he slipped into the gap. He couldn't tell if Hannibal had heard what Todd had said, but with his head down he crawled after Jasper.

He'd covered twenty feet when shuffling sounded behind him. He looked over his shoulder and saw that the marshal was following him.

He ignored the distraction and crawled on. The light ahead disappeared quickly, forcing him to slow down for fear of banging into the sides of the low tunnel.

136

The terrain became rougher when he crawled across rock and the slope became more pronounced. He felt that the sides were closing in on him, and he confirmed that impression when he reached a corner.

He had halved the distance to Jasper and the tunnel ahead was long, stretching beyond the Lonesome Trail and going far below ground level. He recalled the map he had guarded carefully, one that miners had made long before New Town had grown up and which Jasper and others had wanted to study.

In the last few years he had explored the tunnels only once, and then for only a short distance. Without the miners working down there, he had found the quietness intimidating.

He couldn't remember this tunnel, but he remembered the large tunnel into which it presumably opened up, along with the massive cavern that was close by.

He figured that this space was the right place to confront Jasper, so he kept back, maintaining his current distance behind him of thirty feet. He judged that they were beyond the saloon when Jasper looked over his shoulder and saw him.

Jasper crawled on more frantically and Norton stopped to look back. Hannibal was closer. He was on his side, dragging his broken leg behind him.

Norton watched him for a minute to ensure he wasn't planning to take a pot shot at him, then he moved on. He came to a sudden halt.

The lamp was still in the middle of the tunnel, but Jasper had gone. Then a hand came into view from the side of the tunnel and dragged the lamp away, plunging Norton into darkness.

Behind him Hannibal cursed while Norton summoned up an image of the route ahead. Then he fast-crawled along, getting closer to the reflected light cast by the out-of-sight lamp within a minute.

Cold air blasted his face. When he looked towards the light he saw that his quarry had moved into a wide space that was high enough for him to stand.

Norton reckoned he was in the tunnel he'd explored before. He jumped down into it and then stood confidently watching Jasper drag himself along the ground twenty feet away.

Jasper speeded his frantic clawing motion, showing that he'd heard him approach. Then he pressed his head against the rock, as he clearly judged that he couldn't reach wherever he was going before Norton caught up with him.

'Go away, Norton,' he said, shuffling round to face him. 'Your role is to keep my wife amused. This doesn't concern you.'

'It does now.'

Norton gave the gun at his hip a significant glance, but that made Jasper smile.

'She's sent better men than you after me – not that they're hard to find – and yet I'm still alive. What makes you think you'll succeed?'

'Are you saying you killed Ogden Reed?'

Jasper waved a dismissive hand at him before looking down the tunnel and taking a deep breath as he prepared to resume his journey.

'That's far enough,' Hannibal's strident voice said from further down the tunnel.

Norton turned to find that Hannibal was standing with his splinted leg thrust out and one hand pressed to the tunnel wall to keep him upright.

'I'm in control here,' Norton snapped. 'You two will deal with me first.'

Hannibal considered him with the same level of contempt as Jasper had. Then with a sudden movement he drew his gun, the weapon coming to hand before Norton could even react. He aimed at his chest.

'That's a good point.' He gestured with the gun down the tunnel. 'Help that half-man or we'll never get there.'

Reckoning he had no choice, Norton put his hands beneath Jasper's armpits and dragged him to a sitting position. At first Jasper resisted, but another grunted demand from Hannibal made him relent.

Then, at a slow pace, they moved down the tunnel.

Norton dragged Jasper backwards while Hannibal hobbled along with one hand on the wall. With time to think about why Hannibal and Jasper were at loggerheads, Norton's thoughts returned to Todd's comments.

'You're both looking for the same thing down

here, aren't you?' he said. Neither of them replied and so he persisted. 'You both wanted my map and you both claimed you'd been injured in the same place, one after last year's raid on the train and the other after Ogden Reed got shot up.'

The last comment made Hannibal stop.

'I don't have to explain myself to you.'

'You don't, but then again you hoped you'd never have to explain yourself to anyone. Rick Cody was a good deputy, but he might have worked things out. So you sacked him and replaced him with an idiot.'

'Be careful what you say about my son,' Jasper muttered, 'even when it's true.'

'I will, because I know he's no fool. He figured it out first.'

The accusation was enough to make Hannibal point angrily at him.

'One more comment like that,' he snapped, 'and you'll never leave this place.'

Hannibal transfixed him with his gaze, then looked past him, making Norton turn. He flinched. He was only a few paces away from the end of the tunnel and it opened out into a large space.

Curiously, a faint light was ahead and people were moving around. And they were fighting.

CHAPTER 15

Rick hammered a gunshot into the chest of the first man to come onto the ledge, making him double over and drop to the ground, but two more men quickly followed.

These men already had their guns drawn and aimed low. With a futile feeling in his guts, Rick turned to them, but Logan ripped out two quick gunshots, making both men stumble and giving Rick enough time to sight the nearer man.

Before he could shoot, both men fell over, clutching bloodied sides. One man hit the wall while the second man knocked into Rick, sending him reeling.

As he fell he twisted, uncertain of how close to the edge of the rock he was. He was pleased he'd reacted quickly as he fell onto solid rock, but the drop down to the water-filled cavern was only a hand's width away.

The wounded man landed sprawled over on his side while the second man rebounded from the wall before he fell lifelessly over the edge. As gunfire erupted again, Rick watched him crash down into the water.

Determined to avoid that fate, he shoved aside the man who was pinning him down. Then he holstered his gun and rolled, but he struggled to move. Worse, the rock beneath him felt as if it were falling away, a sensation that proved to be justified when a thud sounded.

He fell, a crack in the rock opening up four feet from his outstretched hands. With little hope of saving himself, he scrambled forward, but the rock was already at too steep an angle for him to make progress. Then he stopped moving with a lurch that smashed his face against the ledge.

While holding his breath he saw that a stretch of rock had split away at the side of the ledge. It had fallen for several feet and then caught against the cavern wall.

Logan was shouting something while others shouted back. Rick couldn't hear the words, but the tone was threatening.

Scuffing sounded and the wounded man glanced over the edge, having clearly dragged himself to safety. Then he darted back, using high kicking steps that showed he reckoned the ledge was in a precarious position.

The fallen stretch of rock shifted again, with a worrying scraping sound. When he jerked to a halt Rick clung on until he was sure the ledge had stopped moving. Then he stretched out an arm and patted around until he found a handhold a foot above his head. He used that to draw himself higher.

Another upward movement let him reach the crumbling section, so he strained his biceps to raise himself and lie over the crack. The rock shuddered as he folded his upper body onto the ledge.

He kicked down, but his feet trod only on air. He froze and a few moments later a heavy thud sounded below as the dislodged slab of rock hit the ground. Rick rested his weight on his arms and then twisted, gaining the ledge.

He leapt to his feet and faced the tunnel entrance. On the opposite side of the ledge Logan was slugging it out with two men. A still and bloodied man lay at his feet. Between him and the entrance, Edison and Hedley were trying to wrestle each other to the ground.

Three men had spread out across the entrance, ensuring that nobody could escape while they waited for an opening. When they saw that Rick had survived, they jerked round to face him.

Rick scrambled for his gun, but the men stayed their fire when Edison delivered a swinging blow to Hedley's chin that made him stumble backwards into the space between them. Edison then looked around and, seeing that the tunnel entrance was blocked, he moved in the only direction open to him by running to the end of the ledge.

Edison speeded up, showing he intended to

attempt the seemingly impossible leap to the tunnel on the other side of the cavern. He'd covered half the distance to the end of the ledge when with a grunt of anger the wounded man raised his gun and shot him in the back.

Edison stumbled on for two paces before he slammed down, to lie prone on the ledge. He didn't move again.

Everyone stared at his body, Hedley looking as shocked as everyone else that one of his men had been forced to dispose of Edison.

Logan was the first man to get his wits about him. He slugged his first opponent aside, sending him skittering over the edge of the rock, and knocked over the second man with a well-aimed kick. Then he turned to Hedley, but he had already aimed his gun at Logan while the men in the entrance turned their guns on Rick.

'Did Edison talk?' Hedley asked.

Logan said nothing, his expression thunderous now that his chances of getting to the truth about who had killed his brother had disappeared with Edison's death.

'You mean,' Rick said when it became clear Logan wouldn't speak, 'about the missing silver?'

Hedley nodded and cast an aggrieved glare at the man who had shot Edison, which promised retribution later.

'Edison was supposed to take it to a safe place while we holed up, but he hid it somewhere that only he knew about. You have one chance to convince me that you know what he did with it.'

Rick considered his options, then reached into his pocket. The gunmen tensed, but they smiled when he withdrew a handful of coins and threw them to the ground.

The coins rolled, catching the light, and Hedley trapped one beneath a boot. He raised the boot and gave a low whistle.

'That interest you?' Rick asked.

Hedley worried the coin from side to side with the toe of his boot, his expression pensive as he clearly considered the impending stand-off where they'd trade freedom for information. Rick used the hiatus to try to catch Logan's eye, but Logan was still standing in a hunched and defeated posture.

'Tell me about the rest,' Hedley said, raising his gun to sight Logan's head, 'with no tricks, or I'll blast a hole in your friend.'

Rick reckoned the bags of silver would still be visible below, but showing them to Hedley would relinquish his only advantage. So he sought a distraction to give Logan time to get over his anger by again moving slowly for his pocket.

He withdrew the map and held it up for Hedley to see.

'We used this map,' he said. 'It shows where the rest of the silver is.'

Hedley licked his lips and smirked.

'Then hand it over and you two can go free.'

145

Rick knew the promise was a hollow one. He lowered the map and, while he balanced it on the palm of his hand, from the corner of his eye he considered Logan, who with a shake of his head looked up, apparently acknowledging the danger they faced.

Rick reckoned that was the best reaction he could hope for. He swung his hand back and forth twice before launching the map towards Hedley, but deliberately he threw it low and weakly.

Hedley reacted without thinking and jerked his hand down to pluck the map from the air. At that moment Logan threw his hand to his gun and then twisted at the hips.

Rick, crouching, followed Logan's lead. He was a moment behind Logan in reacting and before his gun had cleared leather Logan fired at the nearest man. His gunshot sliced into the gunman's neck, dropping him. Then Logan fanned a rain of deadly fire across the rest of Hedley's men.

The second man went down with his hand rising to clutch a high, reddening chest wound; the third man got a shot in the centre of his chest that made him fold over and drop to his knees. As Logan moved to take on the remaining two gunmen, Rick swung his gun up. He sighted Hedley and, while his target was still distracted by Logan's onslaught, he fired.

Rick's quick draw caused him to aim badly; his gunshot caught Hedley a glancing blow to the upper arm, making him jerk up his hand, sending the map

146

fluttering upwards.

The pain of the wound made Hedley swing round. He stood still for a moment. Then with a roar of defiance he swung back, his gun in hand and his uninjured arm rising to pick Rick out.

Rick fired again, this time taking careful aim. He blasted an accurate and deadly shot between Hedley's eyes that cracked his head back. Hedley stood, his neck arched, looking up at the map, which had caught an eddy of wind and was spiralling above him.

Then Hedley toppled backwards and clattered down on his back to lie still while the map fluttered back and forth before coming to rest on his chest.

Rick couldn't help but smile when he saw that the paper had landed with the map on the bottom and the wanted poster uppermost. He hadn't noticed before that Todd had drawn the map on a copy of Hedley's own wanted poster.

He shook away the thought that maybe Todd had done this deliberately, and turned to see how Logan was faring. Another gunman lay on his back after Logan had planted a slug in his forehead. Only the wounded man had survived the onslaught and he was doing what he'd stopped Edison from doing: beating a retreat down the ledge.

Logan followed his progress with his gun, but he didn't fire, so Rick let the man go too. With a hand clutched to his side the man speeded up to a sprint until it was impossible for him to stop.

Then he kicked off from the edge and leapt.

As the gunman moved on with his arms waving and his legs wheeling, Rick thought he would achieve the impossible and reach the safety of the tunnel. Then his momentum died out.

He dropped away from the entrance and slammed into the rock face ten feet below his target. A pained grunt sounded as he fell.

A moment later a splash sounded, followed strangely by a loud crack. Logan looked at Rick, his eyebrows raised in a silent question. When the ledge shook, Rick didn't need to answer.

Both men struggled to keep their footing. Then a stronger tremor made them go to their knees.

As the ledge shook and a crack opened across the tunnel entrance Logan gained his feet and ran towards the end. Rick shouted at him to stop, but his voice only appeared to spur Logan on.

Logan reached the end, sprinting faster than the wounded man had managed. Then he launched himself high into the air.

Rick was minded to go for the tunnel entrance instead, but then he saw what must have swayed Logan's decision. A boulder set into the wall above the entrance was shaking loose. Then it dropped.

Before the boulder landed, Rick turned to the end of the ledge. Then he kicked off, setting off so fast he almost slammed face first into the rock, but with his head down he ran on.

As the boulder crashed down behind him and sent

tremors racing down the ledge, Logan landed feet first in the tunnel entrance. Then his momentum carried him past three men, who struggled to get away from his tumbling form.

Rick recognized the newcomers, but he put aside his curiosity about why they'd come down here and concentrated on his own desperate attempt to save himself.

Unlike his earlier failed attempt, Logan had leapt high and Rick decided to use the same method. But, with every pace, leaping higher than the target of the tunnel felt harder as the tunnel appeared to be rising above him.

He glanced down and realized with a start that his perspective had been wrong: the ledge was tipping downwards.

Then it was too late for him to do anything other than to leap in hope.

He reached the end of the ledge and threw himself as high into the air as he could. His forward momentum was strong enough to hurtle him across the gap towards the cavern wall.

Unfortunately, the tunnel was above him and beyond his reach.

Then, with a bone-crunching thud, he slammed into the rock wall, feeling as if he were the silver coin Hedley had crushed beneath his boot.

He began to fall, but only for a moment. His arm caught on something.

His awkward position sent a bolt of pain coursing

from wrist to shoulder. He still deemed himself lucky and, when he looked up, he saw that Logan had leaned out of the tunnel entrance to grab his wrist while he himself hung on to the dangling rope.

For the next few seconds, as bone-rattling thuds sounded from the ledge crashing to the ground, Rick shifted position to reduce the strain on his arm. Then, with his free hand, he held the rope and supported his weight so that Logan could drag him up.

After a few tugging movements Logan deposited him in the tunnel entrance. Both men rolled over onto flat ground and breathed out relieved sighs while ruefully rubbing their bruises.

When Rick looked up he faced Marshal Hannibal, along with Norton Wells and Jasper Snyder. All three men packed guns and, by the light of the lamp Jasper was clutching, their expressions were tense.

Rick felt too sore to wonder what their problem was. Groaning, he crawled along and took refuge sitting back against the tunnel wall. From there he looked down at the water which, after the ledge had fallen, was swirling around and hitting the cavern sides.

'What are you doing down here?' Logan demanded after he had recovered from his exertions.

Norton lowered his head while Jasper and Hannibal shot glances at each other. Then they ignored him and moved on towards the edge.

Hannibal sported a pained look that suggested

he'd banged his leg; so he could manage only a shuffling gait that inched him along, letting Jasper reach the entrance first, despite using only his arms to move.

The light from his raised lamp cast a glow down onto the cavern bottom and, although he wasn't interested in the fate of the silver, Rick still looked for it. Under the stronger light, he saw that the debris of the ledge had created a large mound at the back of the cavern.

Although he judged this was twenty yards from the bags of silver, he couldn't see them. A body was swirling, suggesting that the water was deep enough to have covered the bags. When the current sent the body down the underground stream, Rick reckoned they might also have been carried away.

Jasper's shocked expression as he considered the scene and Hannibal's anger made Rick nod.

'You two,' he said, 'knew about the silver down there.'

'Be quiet,' Jasper muttered. He put the lamp down and dragged his upper body forward so that he could look straight down.

Norton snorted a laugh and moved forward.

'Your nephew,' he said, 'worked out that they were after something.'

His comment made Jasper and Hannibal snarl with anger. They turned to each other and glared into each other's eyes. Then they lunged for each other's throat, but, both men being incapacitated, their assaults were ineffectual.

They fell against each other. Then they gripped each other's neck and strained while anger made their eyes bulge. Hannibal lashed out with his uninjured leg and knocked the lamp over, sending it tumbling into the cavern.

As the light dropped away, their expressions darkened. Then both men unbalanced, toppling to the side before they followed the lamp out through the tunnel entrance.

With their hands around each other's throat, neither man could stay his movement, forcing the closest men, Norton and Logan, to try to save them. Norton lunged for Jasper's right arm, catching his wrist, while Logan grabbed Hannibal's jacket.

Jasper's weight dragged Norton down onto his chest while Logan went to his knees as he strained to hold Hannibal up. Rick figured that Norton was in the most trouble, so he slipped between the two men to help Norton.

As the lamp burst open, he extended an arm. He couldn't reach Jasper's left wrist, so he dangled his hand in Jasper's eye-line. Jasper ignored him and glared at Norton.

'So now you can do my wife's bidding,' he said as flames spread across the surface of the water. 'But are you man enough to do it?'

'I'm saving your life,' Norton muttered, 'not taking it.'

Jasper sneered. 'I'm half a man, but you're even

less. If you're all she can attract now, she's fallen even further than I will.'

He glanced at Rick's hand and then shook himself. His rapid motion tore his wrist from Norton's precarious grip and he dropped.

The flaming surface below ripped apart as Jasper crashed down head first in its centre.

With the flickering flames lighting his troubled gaze, Norton turned to Rick.

'He made me drop him,' he said. 'Why would he do that?'

Rick reckoned that, in an odd way, Jasper had beaten his wife by refusing to let her kill him; that, by choosing his time, he'd left her with a man whom he considered beneath him. He kept those thoughts to himself and slapped an encouraging hand on Norton's shoulder.

Then he turned to the other man who needed rescuing. Logan had a firm grip of Hannibal's jacket with one hand while he'd put his other hand under the marshal's armpit, supporting his weight.

'Why were you fighting with Jasper?' Logan demanded.

When Hannibal's only response was to grunt with anger, Norton overcame his shock and spoke up.

'Edison dropped too many hints about him stealing the silver,' he said. 'But Jasper had already found it. When he hid it elsewhere, he broke himself in two, but after the poker game—'

'I don't care about poker or the silver,' Logan

snapped, his muscles bunching from supporting the dangling marshal. 'I just want to know who killed my brother.'

'Marshal Hannibal killed him to stop him following Edison down here, but he broke his leg while searching.'

Logan nodded, smiling thinly. Then he peered down at Hannibal until he met his gaze.

The two men looked at each other. Then Logan opened his hands and Hannibal dropped; he fell for only a moment, then, with a frantic waving of his arms, he grabbed the trailing end of the rope.

Hannibal hung on one-handed while with his other hand he reached for his gun, but he didn't get to touch leather. Logan drew his gun and calmly aimed downwards.

A single shot rang out. A moment later a splash sounded below.

'I knew,' Logan said, holstering his gun, 'I'd get to the truth in the end.'

CHAPTER 16

Light was spreading across the arc of the eastern horizon when Rick, Logan and Norton headed out of the Lonesome Trail. They stood on the boardwalk enjoying the open air for several minutes until Virginia emerged to ask the question Rick didn't want to answer.

'Is anyone else coming out?' she said.

Rick was still struggling to reply when Norton spoke up.

'We're the only ones who survived,' he said. 'Your husband died down there, as did Edison Dent, Marshal Hannibal, Hedley Beecher, and the rest of his men.'

Virginia lowered her head and had the grace to speak with a gruff voice.

'I'll explain what happened to Todd when I reckon he can cope.'

'He's more capable than you think he is. I'm sure he figured out that Marshal Hannibal killed Ogden

155

Reed and what Hannibal and Jasper were doing down there.'

Virginia looked sceptical, but Rick nodded as he remembered the map on the wanted poster.

'And possibly,' he said, 'what Hedley's plans were, too.'

'Are you saying he has a future as a deputy?' she asked.

Rick looked at the growing light that would mark the end of his duty to this town.

'He has more of a future here,' he said, 'than I have.'

'With Hannibal gone, the town will need a new marshal.'

Rick smiled. Only Hannibal knew that his duty had ended and, when the truth came out about the marshal's actions, he would be in a good position to stay on.

'If that man turns out to be me, I guess I'll need a deputy.'

Virginia sighed and looked past him at the lightening sky.

'I assume you hate me even more now.'

'You didn't kill Ogden Reed or your husband. That's the important thing for me and I hope you can reconcile what you planned to do with your conscience.'

Rick could have said more, but Norton moved between them. He jabbed a finger against Rick's chest.

'Don't be rude to her,' he said. 'She's done nothing wrong.'

'When compared to what others did, plotting to kill your husband is nothing.' Rick chuckled. 'Hopefully that'll let you sleep easy at night.'

Although Norton narrowed his eyes, he couldn't have detected the implied warning as he tried to take Virginia's arm, but Virginia bade him to go back to the saloon alone. When he left, she considered Rick.

'I hope one day you'll forgive me. It was awful being tied to a man you hated even before the lure of the silver broke him in half.' When Rick didn't reply, she turned to Logan. 'But your brother was no better. He abandoned me for the silver too.'

Logan sneered, appearing as if he'd retort to her harsh words, but then with a shake of the head he moved away down the boardwalk.

'As you can see,' Rick said, 'he doesn't want to hear you speak ill of him.'

'Then maybe later I'll tell him the other side of the story: about what Ogden meant to me.'

Rick leaned towards her and lowered his voice.

'Do it when Norton's not around.' When she smiled, Rick smiled in return. 'Are you really going to make a new life with him?'

She shrugged, although the twinkle in her eye confirmed she knew how unlikely this turn of events was.

'I don't want to run the Lonesome Trail on my own and a man like Norton, who cares only for me,

157

might be what I need now.'

'True.' Rick raised an eyebrow. 'But Norton Wells?'

'Don't be rude.' She licked her lips and then winked. 'But in case it doesn't work out, say nice things about me to Logan.'

She gave him a winning smile, then turned to her saloon. Rick watched her until she went inside. Then he moved on to join Logan.

'Your sister might not have killed my brother,' Logan said after a while, 'but she probably knew about the silver and that means she didn't help the situation, did she?'

'Nope.'

Logan tightened his hands into fists, then slowly opened them again, seemingly dismissing his anger.

'Then I reckon I'll move on.'

'Where will you go?'

'As Ogden wanted the silver, I'll head downriver and see if I can find where it washes up.'

Rick smiled. 'To find it, you'll need some local knowledge.'

When Logan nodded, Rick fished a silver coin out of his pocket. He tossed it in the air, caught it on his palm, and then turned it over onto the back of his hand.

'What's the choice?' Logan asked.

'Eagle, I join you in your search for the silver. Liberty, I stay here, make peace with my sister, and be a lawman.'

158

Rick raised his hand, but he didn't look at the coin, leaving Logan to reveal the result.

'Liberty,' he said.

Rick considered the saloon and then turned to look around the rest of the town. He frowned.

'Close enough. Come on. The silver can't have gone far.'